No ordinary mirror . . .

The queen answered my knock in a sleepy voice. When I stepped inside, her eyes were closed, her face unguarded, and she appeared hardly more than ten years old. She sat up and watched me draw her bath, as if she really was a child.

While she soaked, I sat at the dressing table, and I happened to look into the hand mirror.

My reflection began to change. My chalky skin darkened a tone to alabaster. My cheeks turned a pearly pink. My rage-red lips softened to the hue of a ripe strawberry. My pulpy cheeks gained definition. My sooty hair became lustrous. Even my absurd bird headdress looked charming.

Only my eyes were unchanged. I was stunningly beautiful, beautiful beyond any hope I'd ever had.

Also by Gail Carson Levine

Dave at Night

Ella Enchanted

Ever

A Tale of Two Castles

The Two Princesses of Bamarre

The Wish

THE PRINCESS TALES

The Fairy's Mistake

The Princess Test

Princess Sonora and the Long Sleep

Cinderellis and the Glass Hill

For Biddle's Sake

The Fairy's Return

Betsy Red Hoodie

Betsy Who Cried Wolf

Writing Magic: Creating Stories that Fly

Fairy Dust and the Quest for the Egg

Fairy Haven and the Quest for the Wand

fairest

Gail Carson Levine

HARPER

An Imprint of HarperCollinsPublishers

Library of Congress Cataloging-in-Publication Data

Levine, Gail Carson.

Fairest / Gail Carson Levine.— 1st ed.

p.   cm.

Summary: In Ayortha, singing and beauty are prized above all
else. Aza, a commoner, can sing, and Queen Ivi is a beauty. The
queen forces Aza to use her voice to deceive the entire court.

ISBN 978-0-06-073410-7

[1. Fairy tales. 2. Beauty, Personal—Fiction. 3. Singing—
Fiction. 4. Self-acceptance—Fiction. 5. Identity—Fiction.] I. Title.

PZ8.L4793Fa 2006   2006000337

[Fic]—dc22   CIP

                                                    AC

Typography by Larissa Lawrynenko

13   CG/OPM   10   9   8

Revised edition, 2012

To David, who has a chamber in my heart.

To Rosemary Brosnan, who sweetly wields the knife.

ACKNOWLEDGMENT

Many thanks to opera star Janet Hopkins for introducing me, with kindness and encouragement, to the mysteries of singing.

CHAPTER ONE

I was born singing. Most babies cry. I sang an aria.

Or so I believe. I have no one to tell me the truth of it. I was abandoned when I was a month old, left at the Featherbed Inn in the Ayorthaian village of Amonta. It was January 12th of the year of Thunder Songs.

The wench who brought me to the inn paid for our chamber in advance and smuggled me in unseen. The next morning she smuggled herself out, leaving me behind.

I know what happened next. Father and Mother—the innkeeper and his wife—have retold the tale on the anniversary of my arrival since I grew old enough to understand the words.

"You were left in the Lark chamber," Mother would say. "It was the right room for you, my songbird."

"It was a chill morning," Father would chime in. "Soon you were howling." His shoulders would shake with laughter.

"I thought you were Imilli."

We would all smile—my younger sister Areida, my two older brothers, Mother, and I. Imilli was our cat—kitten then.

Mother would burst in. "I knew straight off you were a babe. I knew you were a singer, too." She'd sing, "It was all in your lovely howl."

We'd laugh at that.

She'd shake her head. "No. Truly. It was lovely."

My favorite part would come next. Mother would throw back her head and imitate my howl, a high pure note.

Ayortha is a kingdom of singers. In our family and in Amonta, my voice is the finest. Mother often said that if I tried, I could sing the sun down from the sky.

"I opened the chamber door," Father would say, continuing the tale, "and there you were."

I was in the center of the bed, crying and kicking the air.

"I picked you up," Mother would say, "and you gurgled such a musical gurgle."

My brother Ollo would break in with his favorite part. "Your bottom was wet."

Areida would giggle.

Father and Mother would never mention that the blanket I had arrived in was velvet, edged with gold thread.

The story would go on. Mother carried me into the

Sparrow room, where my brothers slept. Father headed for the attic to find Ollo's old cradle. When he came down, I was lying on Ollo's small bed while Ollo, who was two years old then, gently poked my cheek.

No one has told me what happened next, but I know. I can imagine the sight I was. Yarry, who was five, would have spoken his mind, as he does to this day. He would have said, in a tone of wonder, "She's so ugly."

Then—they *have* told me this—he said, "Can we keep her, Father?"

Father and Mother did, and named me Aza, which means *lark* in Ayorthaian. They treated me no differently from their own children, and taught me to read music and songs from our treasured leather songbook, kept on its own high table in the entry parlor.

I was an unsightly child. My skin was the weak blue-white of skimmed milk, which wouldn't have been so bad if my hair had been blond and my lips pale pink. But my lips were as red as a dragon's tongue and my hair as black as an old frying pan.

Mother always denied that I was ugly. She said that looking different wasn't the same as looking amiss, and she called me her one-of-a-kind girl. Still, she promised I'd grow prettier as I grew older. I remember asking her a dozen times a day if I was prettier yet. She would stop whatever she was doing—cleaning a guest's chamber or bathing Areida—and consider me. Then she'd sing, "I think so."

But soon after, one of the inn's guests would stare, and I'd know the transformation hadn't really taken place.

If anything, I became uglier. I grew large boned and awkward. My chubby cheeks were fine for a babe, but not for an older child. I resembled a snow maid, with a big sphere of a face and round button eyes.

I ached to be pretty. I wished my fairy godmother would come and make me so. Mother said we all have fairy godmothers, but they rarely reveal themselves. I wished I could see mine. I was sure fairies were supremely beautiful and glorious in every way.

Mother said fairy godmothers only watch from afar and sympathize. I didn't see the good of a hand-wringing fairy godmother. I needed one who'd fly in and help.

With no hope for fairy intervention, I wished for a magic spell to make me pretty. At night I'd sing nonsense words to myself after Areida had fallen asleep. I thought I might stumble on the right combination of syllables and notes, but I never did.

I attempted to make myself more presentable by pinning my hair up this way or that, or by tying a ribbon around my neck. Once, I sneaked into Father's workshop and smeared wood stain on my face and arms.

The results were streaky brown skin and a rash that lasted a month.

The inn's guests were sometimes friendly, but more often they were rude. As bad as the ones who stared were the ones who looked away in embarrassment. Some guests didn't want me to serve their food, and some didn't want me to clean their rooms.

We Ayorthaians are sensitive to beauty, more sensitive than the subjects in other kingdoms, I think. We love a fine voice especially, but we also admire a rosy sunset, a sweet scent, a fetching face. And when we're not pleased, we're displeased.

I developed the habit of holding my hand in front of my face when guests arrived, a foolish practice, because it raised curiosity and concealed little.

Mother and Father mostly gave me chores that kept me out of sight, helping the laundress or washing dishes. They did so to protect me. But it was common sense, too. I was bad for business.

Sometimes I wondered if they regretted taking me in, and sometimes I wished I'd been abandoned at a farmhouse. The chickens wouldn't have minded if an ugly maiden fed them. The cows wouldn't have minded if an ugly maiden cleaned their stalls.

Or would they?

CHAPTER TWO

*T*HE ONLY FEATHERBED guests who were comfortable with me were the gnomes. They never stared, never seemed even to notice my appearance.

Gnomes upset the inn's routine. Ettime, our cook, had to prepare root-vegetable stews for them, the only human food gnomes can eat. But Father was glad to have them anyway. Gnomes, at least the ones who traveled, were wealthy. They tipped generously and paid in advance. Better yet, they often paid double, because husbands and wives took separate rooms, since adult gnomes were too wide to share our beds.

Mother always had me serve them and clean their rooms. One day I was polishing the chest of drawers in the Crane chamber when its occupant returned.

I was singing a cleaning song I'd made up and didn't hear him. He stood in the doorway as I sang:

"I'm not a Sir, but a serf,
And my enemy's worse
Than a knight ever cursed.

"My foes are the dirt, the dust,
The filth and decay.
I brandish my mop, my rag,
And my scouring pad.
My enemies flee, or they melt,
Or they die.
But they have friends, and
Their friends have friends,
Who have more friends.
And whatever I try,
The dirt never ends.

"Slime and grime,
Sludge and smudge,
Mud and crud.
Oh, gooey guck.
And gluey muck.
I'm not a Sir, I'm a serf,
And my enemy's worse
Than a knight ever cursed."

The gnome, whose name was zhamM, said, "Oh, my!" I turned, startled, and he was waving his hands in the air, applauding the Ayorthaian way. My blotchy blush began, but his arms didn't come down. I smiled at him.

He smiled back, showing teeth that resembled iron posts. "I like your song. It is charming, to be exact. And your voice is more than charming."

zhamM was a frequent guest at the inn, although we had never spoken to each other before. I thought of him as the green gentleman—*green* because of the emerald buttons on all his tunics, *gentleman* because he was polite and fussy, with a soft, breathy voice and small gestures. He had curly brown hair, small ears set close to his head, and skin almost as pale as my own.

"Shall I leave, Master zhamM?" I said. "I can finish cleaning later." I hoped he'd say no. I had a question I'd long wished to ask a gnome if the opportunity arose.

"No need. I only want to think a moment. To be exact, I can do that as badly with you here as with you gone." He sat carefully on the bench by the fireplace.

How nice he was. I worked slowly. I couldn't ask my question until he finished thinking.

I was changing his pillowcase and deciding to scrub the washstand again when he stood up.

"There," he said. "I am finished thinking, perhaps for the month."

Was he jesting? I smiled uneasily, holding his pillow by a corner.

He nodded, reading my expression. "Yes, it is a jest. Not so humorous, to be exact."

I gathered my courage and said in a rush, "Can you see what's to come?" Some gnomes could.

"Hints, glimmers. We never see more."

I didn't know if a hint or a glimmer would be specific enough. "Would you be so kind . . . would it be too much trouble . . ."

"There's something you'd like to know?"

I blurted out, "Will I ever be pretty?" I hugged the pillow, protecting myself against his answer.

"Never."

"Oh."

He must have seen my misery, because he added, "All humans are ugly, to be exact."

"All humans?"

"Yes."

I was amazed.

He went on. "You are slightly less ugly than most. Your hair is a beautiful color, htun. I've never seen a human with htun hair before."

I wasn't listening. "Will I ever be pretty to people?"

"To humans?" He stared over my left shoulder. I thought

his expression changed, although his face was so leathery and seamed, so lizardlike, I wasn't sure.

A minute passed.

"Maid Aza . . . that is your name?"

I nodded.

"In Gnomic we would call you Maid azacH." He folded his hands across his chest, delivering a pronouncement. "In the future, you and I will meet again."

Even I could see far enough into the future to see that. He stayed at the Featherbed once or twice every month.

"I smelled my home and saw glow iron. To be exact, we'll meet again in Gnome Caverns. You will be in danger."

What sort of danger, and how would I get to Gnome Caverns? But I skipped to my main concern. "Will I look as I do now?"

"You will be smaller. . . ."

Smaller would be a big improvement! "Do your visions always come to pass?"

"This will come to pass, unless you do something irregular at a crossroad."

I didn't understand.

"There was one more change in you in my vision. Your hair was black, with little htun left."

"What's htun?"

"Htun looks black to humans. It is the color I like best,

deeper than scarlet, more serene than cerulean, gayer than yellow. Your htun hair is the most beautiful I've ever seen."

I stared down at the floor, trying not to cry. No one had ever before said that anything about me looked beautiful.

If only humans could see htun.

In the year of Barn Songs, when I was twelve, the duchess of Olixo and her companion, Dame Ethele, stopped at the Featherbed for a night. Father and Mother were thrilled, but also worried. If the duchess liked the inn, she could steer other rich customers to us. If she disliked it, she could get our license revoked by the king.

I was thrilled and worried, too. Thrilled, because I'd never seen a duchess before, and worried, because the duchess had never seen *me* before. I'd stay out of the way, but if our paths crossed, would she hate the sight of me?

I was serving dinner to a party of gnomes when she arrived, earlier than expected, or I would never have been in the tavern. Father conducted a small plump woman and a large one to the best table. The large woman, who was approximately my own size, had more ribbons and bows on her gown than I'd ever seen collected together. The small one was as richly clad, but more simply.

Neither of them glanced my way. I wondered which was duchess and which was companion. It would have been rude to stare, as I knew better than anyone. I stole glances, however, and soon decided who was who. The large one was Dame Ethele, and the small plump one was the duchess.

How did I know?

Well, the small woman's expression was petulant, but the big woman smiled. The smiling one had to be the companion. After all, who would pay to have a petulant companion?

I was perplexed by the duchess's petulance. What did she have to be petulant about? She was a duchess, and she didn't have a face that made dogs howl.

The duchess didn't like her dinner. Ettime had prepared her best dish, hart sautéed with spring onions and Ayorthaian fire peppers.

Unfortunately, the duchess detested peppers of every sort, and she expected everyone to know it. Mother apologized and brought out a double helping of chicken pot pie, but the damage was done. The duchess's frown deepened.

Before she left her table, she told Mother she wanted a mug of hot ostumo delivered to her chamber at nine that night. "Not a second before nine," she said in a voice that carried, "nor yet a second after, but on the stroke itself—or I shall send it back. And it must be piping hot. Piping! Or I shall send it back."

After I finished waiting on the gnomes, I was sent to the stable to help another gnome find a belt buckle in one of his trunks. It was a prolonged business. The buckle, naturally, was in the third and final trunk.

I returned to the kitchen while Ettime was preparing the ostumo, a mixture of grain and molasses that was Ayortha's favorite beverage. She was so flustered by the duchess that she scalded the first pot and had to throw it out.

By five before nine, the second pot was ready. Mother poured it into a mug and placed the mug on a tray.

A crash and a loud oath came from the tavern. Mother turned toward the tavern door. "I'd better . . ." She stopped and turned back to the *piping!* hot mug. She looked appealingly at Ettime.

"Not me, Mistress Ingi. I won't bring anything to that duchess. And I'm no tavern wench."

I wished I was still in the stable. I couldn't settle a tavern brawl, and the duchess wouldn't want to see my face looming over her ostumo.

We heard another crash and more swearing. There was no time to get Father or my brothers.

"Aza . . ." Mother wet her finger and wiped a smudge off my cheek. She tucked a stray strand of hair into my bonnet. "Take the ostumo to the duchess and come—"

"I can't!"

"I've no one else. Come right back and tell me what she says." She put the tray with the no-longer-*piping!*-hot ostumo into my hands.

The clock began to strike nine.

"Hurry!" Mother snatched up the broom and dustpan and marched into the tavern.

I left the kitchen and started up the stairs, although I wanted to hide in the cellar. It will be over in a moment, I told myself. And answered myself, Yes, the duchess will toss the ostumo in my face. Then she'll call for her carriage and leave.

Imilli was snoozing on the stairway landing. I scooped him up. I could hold him high so the duchess would see less of me.

She was in our best room, the Peacock chamber. I knocked on the door.

CHAPTER THREE

THE DUCHESS OPENED HER door. "You're late. Take it away. I—" She saw Imilli. I don't think she noticed me. "Oh, the sweetie." She took him. "Aren't you a sweetie?" She gestured at the ostumo. "Put it next to the bed. I have sweeties at home. Would you like me to tell you their names?"

She was talking to Imilli, but I nodded. She no longer looked petulant. I followed her into the room.

"I have ten sweet cats. Their names are Asha, Eshe, Ishi, Osho, Ushu, Yshy, Alka, Elke . . ."

The duchess didn't seem to have much imagination. I said the next two names in my mind as she spoke them.

". . . Ilki and Olko. Then there are my sweet kittens." She sat on her bed. Imilli leaned against her chest and purred.

I put the ostumo on the night table and backed away.

"I've named only two kittens thus far." She looked at me.

I raised my hand in front of my face.

She went on. "Do you have any suggestions for the rest? Sit down. There are seven in the litter."

I sat on the stool by the washstand.

"Not there. There." She nodded at the chair by the fireplace, where I wouldn't have dared to sit.

I took it. "Perhaps you could name them Anya, Enye, Inyi, Onyo, and Unyo."

"Those are possible. What's this sweetie called?"

"Imilli, Your Grace."

"Ah. Then I will name the rest Amilla and Emille and so on." She tasted her ostumo.

I held my breath.

Her complaining tone was back. "It isn't hot. Moreover, it's weak. The kitchen will have to do better when I come again. Would you like me to tell you which is my favorite sweetie?"

She would come again! I nodded. The duchess told me, and told me which was her second favorite and her third.

Two hours later, wild with worry and curiosity, Mother opened the duchess's door a crack. There was the duchess, snoring in her bed, Imilli curled up in the crook of her arm.

And there I was, sleeping in the duchess's chair.

The duchess became a regular guest at the inn. She

remained fractious and difficult to please, but she adored Imilli and tolerated me.

In the year of Forest Songs, when I was fourteen, I discovered a new way to sing. I was cleaning the Falcon chamber, which had been occupied by a Kyrrian merchant, Sir Peter of Frell.

After I dusted the mantelpiece, I went to the washstand. The basin was there, but not the pitcher. As I sang, "Where is the pitcher?" I began to hiccup.

I sang, "Did Sir Peter"—hiccup—"steal the pitcher?" I knew the tricks of less-than-honorable guests. "But," I sang, "it's very large for stealing."

I opened the top drawer of the bureau. "Empty. Then where is the—" I hiccuped. My next word, *pitcher*, seemed to come from the center of the canopy over the four-poster bed.

The hiccup had flung the word across the room. How odd. I opened the middle bureau drawer. Empty. I opened the bottom drawer.

"Ah-ha!" Shards of pitcher. "Sir Peter"—hiccup—"hid his crime."

An honorable guest would have confessed to breaking the pitcher and would have paid for the damage.

"Sir Peter is a—" I hiccuped again. *Scoundrel* seemed to

issue from the flowerpot on the windowsill.

Hmm. I stopped cleaning and began a love song that was on everyone's lips lately.

> *"From your roses I've won just a—"*

I tried to fling *thorn* from my throat the way the hiccup had flung *scoundrel*, but it wouldn't go. I sounded half strangled instead. I tried again and failed again. I went on with the song.

> *"In your wide eyes, I've seen only scorn.*
> *From your heart song, I've heard but a . . ."*

I hiccuped. *Sigh* emanated from the corner by the door.

I stayed in the Falcon chamber, not cleaning. I couldn't stop trying to fling my voice. My hiccups passed, but I kept trying—and failing.

Mother found me there and scolded me soundly. I didn't tell her what I'd been doing, because it would have sounded ridiculous. I said I'd been woolgathering and returned to work. But from then on, whenever I had a minute of solitude, I tried again.

I knew my stomach had done most of the work, so I pulled it in hard, trying to get enough thrust. For my pains

I gave myself a sore abdomen. Still I kept at it, and sometimes I thought, Almost. Then, after a month, I had my first success. I was cleaning the Dove chamber, and I made the word *apple* sound as if it was coming from the floor two feet from my feet.

Apples were the fruit I liked least, but they were delicious to sing and delicious to fling.

I tried again and failed. But on the next attempt, *apple* rang from the windowsill.

After that I made swift progress. Soon I could send my voice wherever I wanted, within reason. I couldn't send it a mile away.

My next endeavor was to learn to fling my voice without moving my lips. This required weeks of practice, touching my face to make sure it was motionless. I might have progressed faster if I'd looked in a mirror, but I never looked in mirrors.

I named the new skill *illusing*. I was a good mimic, so I added mimicry. Alone in the stable, I learned to illuse Father's voice—speech or singing—and make it come from the hayloft. I could conjure Mother's voice answering from the yard outside, and I could call forth a whinny from an empty stall. I could even duplicate the creak of the stable door when it was opened.

My first demonstration was to Areida, although I hadn't planned it that way.

She and I shared the Hummingbird chamber. Her bedtime was ten, while I was always up until midnight and later, washing dishes while Mother and Father and my brothers cleaned the tavern and prepared for the next day.

It was a Saturday night. The tavern revelers had been boisterous. When the dishes were done I climbed the stairs, weary and angry. A drunken guest had called me an ogress.

If I'd been an ogre, I could have persuaded him I was beautiful. I could have eaten him and made him think he was being caressed by the comeliest maiden in Ayortha. I may have been almost as ugly as an ogre, but I had none of their persuasive powers.

Areida awakened when I came in. She sat up in bed. "Did anything happen? Did we get a new Master Ikulni?"

This was her constant eager question. Master Ikulni was a legendary guest, who'd stayed with us only once, long ago, when Father's grandfather was a boy. As soon as Master Ikulni had arrived, every mirror in the Featherbed shattered. No guest ever ate as much as he did. And the cook never cooked as well, before or after, as she had for him.

Master Ikulni had paid in gold yorthys and tipped lavishly. But every coin melted into air the day after his departure.

Areida craved the excitement of such an interesting guest.

Tonight I had no patience. "Hush. I'm too tired."

"Oh." She plopped back down with a thump.

I undressed to my shift and got into bed next to her. I kept picturing the guest's flushed, foolish face.

"What do you wish?" Areida sang the beginning of a rhyming game.

She was a pest! "Shh! Father will come. I'm too exhausted to sing."

"I'm not," she sang, more softly. "I wish for a moat and a boat and a float."

I wished she'd shut up. I was silent.

"I wish for a twister, a blister, a wide-awake sister."

"If you don't hush I'll smother you." I felt tears coming.

"I wish for—"

"Can't you just this once"—I squeezed my eyes shut. I wouldn't let that taunt make me cry—"stop being a pest?"

"No. I wish—"

"I hate you."

She was silent.

I felt awful. A tear got out. Now I'd made Areida unhappy. "I don't hate you."

She was silent.

A sob got out.

She sat up. "I'm sorry." She patted my shoulder. "I should have guessed."

I raised myself on one elbow. My tears were flowing now. "It's not your fault."

"I despise them."

"They think I don't have feelings." I wiped my eyes on our quilt.

"Can a dragon judge ostumo?"

It was what she always said. It meant that louts had no idea of the finest things.

She added, "You have the most beautiful voice."

"You do, too."

"Not like yours. And you always smell nice. Like fennel seeds."

"Fennel?"

"Fennel. Warm and savory. And your eyes are gorgeous."

"Thank you." My eyes were my only acceptable feature.

"And I wish I was as tall as you. You look like a statue."

I'd have given anything to be as neatly and daintily made as Areida.

"Besides—" Her voice took on an adult tone I disliked. "Besides, how one looks isn't important. You're proof of that."

I was proof looks *were* important. Areida could say they weren't only because she was pretty. But I didn't want to quarrel with her twice in five minutes.

We were quiet.

She said, "I love you."

I touched her arm. "I know."

She settled back down. "Good night."

"Good night." But I wanted to make amends. I illused a tiny mouse voice, coming from the floor near the bed. "I love you, too." I illused a wet fishy voice, coming from the washbasin. "I love you, too."

She popped up. "What . . ."

I illused a dry raspy voice coming from the fireplace. "I love you, too."

"What's making—"

I put her hand on my throat so she could feel the vibration. I illused a chirpy voice above our heads: "I love you, too."

"Tell me what you're doing. Don't just keep doing it."

"All right." I told her about illusing. I put one of her hands back on my throat and one on my stomach while I tried to explain how I did it.

A quarter hour later, I went to sleep, and she stayed up the rest of the night, trying to illuse.

She kept trying for the following week, with no success. At the end of the week, I showed the technique to the rest of the family. None of them could do it, either, although each of them tried to learn.

Mother and Father urged me to illuse at the next village

Sing. They were proud of my voice, and they wanted me to stand out, this once, in a way that was to my advantage.

But I decided to keep my illusing secret. If I revealed it, the villagers would try to learn, too. I'd have to explain how I flung the sound out. I'd have to address them all. Singing to them was easy. Speaking was hard. Worst of all, I'd have to show them how I moved my belly.

It was too mortifying to consider.

CHAPTER FOUR

A FEW MONTHS AFTER I discovered illusing, Mother and Father sent Areida to finishing school in the Kyrrian town of Jenn. Their notion was that a refined young woman would raise the tone of the inn.

I understood. Why spend money on the ugly sister, who stayed out of sight as much as possible? Why spend money on the ugly sister when no amount of finishing would alter her face?

I felt hurt anyway. For a day and a half I hated my family and everyone else. And myself most of all.

Then I forgave them. But I didn't forgive myself.

Areida didn't want to go. She wept as she packed.

I was folding her hose. I sang, "Everything will be mildewed by the time you get there."

She laughed and mopped her tears with a table napkin.

She sang back, "I can't help it. I'll miss you. Nobody hugs the way you do."

"You'll have too many new friends to miss anybody." I illused a succession of creatures from different parts of the room, singing, "Have fun at finishing school," and "I'll be waiting for you," and "I love you."

When I was fifteen, in the year of Kitchen Songs, in the month of April, King Oscaro announced his betrothal to a commoner from the Kyrrian town of Bast. She was the daughter of a wealthy silversmith. Her name was Ivy—Ivi in Ayorthaian. She was nineteen, and the king was forty-one. She'd never visited Ayortha. The king had met her in Bast and had conducted his courtship there.

She was a mystery and would remain so until the wedding ceremony. We have a superstition: From betrothal to wedding, alter nothing, or the marriage will be cursed. Ivi wasn't to arrive at Ontio Castle until the day before the wedding, and only her own servants from Bast would wait on her until she was wed.

The nobility were scandalized that she was a commoner. Everyone but me was outraged by her youth and her foreignness.

I felt a connection to the bride, another outsider. I thought of her often, and spoke to her in my imagination, calling her *Ivi*—not *Queen Ivi*, as she would be, but *Ivi*, as if we were intimate friends. I was sure she had a voice beyond compare and the fairest face I'd ever seen.

Our village tailor had a cousin in Bast. We learned that Ivi was high-spirited. She had a temper and was a great flirt. The tailor said she was "nothing extraordinary to look at, merely pretty."

To me, *merely* and *pretty* were words that had nothing to do with each other. *Pretty* went with *miraculously*, and *merely* belonged in another paragraph entirely.

But the most important question, the question on everyone's lips, went unanswered. The tailor's cousin didn't know what sort of voice the bride had. People in Kyrria didn't break into song as we did. They had dances—balls—rather than Sings.

Ayorthaians have been singers from the earliest days of the kingdom. There is hardly a mediocre singer among us. Legend has it that our first king, King Odino, sang in his castle garden, and up sprang the first Three Tree, the symbol of our kingdom.

We believe singing has power—to call forth a tree, to heal the sick, even to move the stars.

Feeling moves us to song. Ideas can move us to song. Even long vowels may move us to song. A sentence like *They may stay away today* is likely to be sung. Our ceremonies are conducted in song. We hold monthly Sings, and we call Sings for healing, for guidance, for settling arguments.

Invitations to King Oscaro's wedding were sent to the nobility, to influential commoners, and to dignitaries from Kyrria. The duchess was invited, naturally, and she and Dame Ethele stopped at the Featherbed on their way to the wedding. Dame Ethele had a cold, and a cold before a royal wedding is a near tragedy. One can't sing well with a cold.

By morning Dame Ethele was too ill to leave the inn. The duchess told Father to call in a physician. Then she had me help her dress for her journey alone to the royal castle.

"It is a trial to have a sickly companion," she said as I laced up her corset.

"Mmm, Your Grace," I said diplomatically.

"People will criticize me for traveling alone. But I don't keep a spare companion. No one does." She stepped into her farthingale. "Fetch my bodice." She sang, "Imilli looks thin."

"He's growing old, Your Grace." I held out the bodice.

"Old! He's not old. Help me with the hooks."

I began to do so.

"Have you grown taller? I believe you've surpassed Ethele."

"Your skirt next, Your Grace?"

She looked at me appraisingly. "Ethele's gowns would fit you."

Occasionally guests gave cast-off clothing to Mother. Dame Ethele's gowns were clownish. I demurred. "Thank you, but—"

"Not to keep! To wear to the wedding."

"Whose wedding, Your Grace?"

"Aza! I thought you were less thickheaded than most peasants."

"I'm sorr—" I gasped. "The king's wedding? Your Grace, the king's wedding!"

I was terrified. There would be hundreds of strangers at the castle, hundreds of staring strangers who'd never encountered anyone as ugly as I was.

But I wanted to see Ivi and the king and hear the singing. The singing at a royal wedding would be superb. And the duchess said there would be a Sing the night after the wedding as well. I'd hear every voice at court when they sang their solos.

Mother and Father agreed to let me go. Indeed, they could hardly refuse the duchess, and they were excited for me. Both of them, and my brothers as well, came out to the coach to send me off.

Mother said I mustn't miss a single detail at the castle. "Your sister will want to hear about the fashions. And

I"—she looked embarrassed—"should like to hear about the hairstyles."

Father said, "Pay attention to how they run the place, daughter. A castle is just a grand inn."

Ollo said, "Sing loud, Aza. Let the king hear the Featherbed's royal voice."

I blushed.

Yarry said, "Don't fret. The way you sing, you could look worse than you do, and it wouldn't matter."

"Yarry!" Mother said.

"I only meant—"

"Hush, son." Father took four copper yorthys from his pocket. He sang, "In a castle it's fine to have a purse that jingles."

I was close to tears. Father was so kind. I'd never had so much as a tin yorthy before. I put the coins in my reticule.

The footman handed the duchess and me into the carriage. Mother waved her dish towel.

The carriage door closed. The duchess leaned back against a brocade seat. "It's a shame you're so . . ." She trailed off, then resumed, on Yarry's theme. "With your voice, if you were pretty, this trip might be the making of you."

CHAPTER FIVE

As we rode in the carriage toward Ontio Castle, the duchess talked about cats and I darned hose from the basket she handed me. We stopped for the night at an inn where both the beds and the porridge were lumpy. The innkeeper stared at me, as rude as any of the Featherbed guests.

In the morning the road became steeper as we entered the foothills of the Ormallo mountain range. The slopes were dotted with boulders.

Ontio Castle was halfway up Mount Ormallo, the highest peak in the range. Gnome Caverns was somewhere beneath the mountains. I thought of the gnome zhamM's prediction that I'd see him there—and that I'd be in danger. The prediction still seemed preposterous, but I was nearer to his home than I'd ever been.

The carriage rounded a bend. There was the castle,

popping out above us, the famed ivy even greener than I expected.

I had been taught the castle had sixteen towers, five square and eleven round. I felt them eyeing us, and I wondered if they were feeling friendly or hostile. If friendly, I hoped they wouldn't change their minds when they saw me up close.

The carriage clattered across the drawbridge. I saw swans swimming in the moat, four white and one black. The carriage stopped. I heard birdsong and people singing. A footman in royal livery helped the duchess step down. I jumped out after her.

A tall Three Tree stood guard by the entrance. The duchess went in, along with the coachman and two footmen, each bearing a trunk. I hugged my carpetbag and followed behind.

Inside the Great Hall, I stopped. The birdsong was louder here. I looked up. An exaltation of larks flew overhead, beneath a ceiling that seemed as distant as the heavens. A troubadour near the doors played his lute and sang an Ayorthaian nonsense song. I stopped to listen and gawk.

"The wind took my hat,
My jig-prancing favorite hat
With its leap-feather whim

> *And its whirling adoring*
> *Red heather."*

A juggler sang along while keeping seven silver sticks in the air.

> *"I whirred at my cat,*
> *My faint-speckled chocolate cat.*
> *In my wish-whether well. . . ."*

Four courtiers watched the juggler. A peasant woman held a tray of chestnut candies and waited for customers. A falconer stood with a hooded bird strapped to his wrist.

My eyes were drawn to the courtiers. Three were women, slouching with their hips thrust forward. Mother would have thought their posture dreadful, but I found it worldly and appealing. I thrust my own hips out and immediately felt ridiculous. I drew them back in.

Areida was prettier than any of the women. I was uglier.

"Aza!"

I hurried after the duchess, still gawking.

My bedchamber was only slightly less grand than the duchess's. My bedposts were mahogany, and the fringe on the canopy was three inches long!

We had rugs at the Featherbed, but ours were worn to frayed thread. Here, the rugs were new and springy and the patterns were bright. I had four rugs. They were small, to be sure, but four!

I took off my travel-worn gown and draped the skirts over the dressing-table mirror. Then I went to the wash-stand, which was marble, so cool and smooth I had to stroke it. I poured water from the pitcher into the basin. A small sculpture stood in the soap dish. The sculpture was of a green dragon, the size of a goose egg. Its mouth was open, but no carved flames spewed out. It was singing, not flaming.

But where was the soap? Surely they washed with soap here. Perhaps the washstand had a lower shelf. I bent down. No shelf.

Reading this, you know what a bumpkin I was. But the truth finally arrived. Smiling with delight, I picked up the dragon and scratched its scales. Soap flakes. The dragon *was* the soap.

After I washed, I dressed in the ensemble of Dame Ethele's that the duchess had told me to wear. The under-shirt was white silk embroidered with yellow roses. Lovely. I slipped it over my head. It settled on me like soft rain.

That was the end of my pleasure. Dame Ethele's hose was no better than the thick cotton stockings I'd left at home.

The gray bodice was tight around my chest, although the shoulders were puffed. I struggled for air and wished I could breathe through my shoulders.

Above the bodice, I tied on a starched white ruff. The stays jabbed into my neck. I stepped into a farthingale with hoops wide enough to encircle a haystack. Over the farthingale went a green underskirt and then a pleated tan overskirt edged with fur.

"I expect you to wear both skirt and underskirt," the duchess had said. "I won't have you scantily clad."

Scantily! It would take a carpenter a month to drill through the skirts and find my legs.

I examined the headdress. The top part was stiff, rough textured, and dark gray, resembling a roof shingle. A broad strip of white linen had been glued to it. I put the headpiece on, tied the linen behind my head, and pushed the ends under the ruff. I was perspiring. I felt pinched here and pricked there, but I was dressed.

I had to see how I looked. I whipped the skirts off the mirror. Then I tilted it to see as much of my reflection as possible. I looked—

And burst into tears.

CHAPTER SIX

I LOOKED LIKE A cottage, with my doughy face peeking out from under the roof. Hundreds of people were going to see me, and I looked even uglier than I truly was.

I sat on the bed. I couldn't stop crying, although I knew the duchess was waiting.

She barged in. A cat rode on her shoulder. Until then I had never seen her laugh. But now she tittered. The titters turned to gales, then shrieks of laughter.

"Not . . . laughing . . . at you . . ." she had the grace to gasp out. "The . . . bonnet!"

I couldn't laugh along. I waited her out.

When she recovered, she allowed me to wear a different headdress. She told me she had something that would do. She left and returned, holding a gray cap with a single gray feather. "I never thought I'd wait on a servant," she said, handing it to me.

The cap was better. The gown was still absurd, but I was no longer quite so conspicuous.

After I helped her dress, we joined the crowd trooping through the castle corridors. I shortened my stride to the duchess's mincing steps. Enough people stared at me to make me wish myself back in my room. I thought of my family. If I missed the wedding, so would they.

We finally reached the Hall of Song, which I'd heard of for as long as I could remember. Oaken pillars supported an oaken ceiling. Each pillar was a wooden elongated singer whose lines and features had been softened by the centuries. Suspended from the ceiling a wooden winged singer flew, her lips forming an O. A living lark perched on her left hand. Its song, clear and fine, was enhanced by the hall's legendary acoustics.

The seats were arranged in a three-quarter circle facing a stage. The duchess's rank commanded a seat in the first row. I was on her right. Everyone was standing, and we stood, too.

A tiny man with bushy eyebrows stood between the stage and the seats. He held a baton, so I knew he must be Sir Uellu, the Ontio choirmaster, the most respected person in Ayortha after the king.

A flutist waited next to Sir Uellu, who raised his baton. The flutist began to play. Everyone hummed along with the flute. Under cover of the other voices, I illused, so that my humming came from the mouth of the wooden singer overhead. I was certain no one would hear me, but the choirmaster looked up. My heart almost flew out my mouth. I stopped illusing.

King Oscaro and Prince Ijori and a large black boarhound stepped through the wine-red velvet curtains at the back of the stage. I knew the king by his crown and the prince by his dog. Every Ayorthaian knew about the prince and his faithful hound, Oochoo.

Prince Ijori was only seventeen, but he was taller than his uncle, the king. He had his uncle's rounded cheeks and narrow chin. He was handsome, very handsome, but for overlarge ears. I liked those ears. They were whimsical. They were charming.

The prince's expression was solemn, but I detected a gleam in his eye. Then I saw Oochoo lick a tidbit out of his hand. The hand moved to the pocket of his tunic, and the dog got another treat.

The king was smiling, and I saw why everyone loved him. His smile was so sweet and kindly. King Oscaro was said to have the best heart in the kingdom. I believed it.

He stepped to the edge of the stage while Prince Ijori and Oochoo moved to the side.

A latecomer, a middle-aged woman wearing a gold tiara,

crossed in front of me to reach her place three seats away. I wondered if she was Princess Elainee, the prince's mother, the king's sister.

I sensed eyes on me. I glanced up, and it was the prince. I felt my blotchy blush begin. I saw myself in my mind's mirror. Blushing made me as garish as blood on snow.

I felt the duchess turn. I turned, too, as the bride entered the hall. The flutist missed a measure. Everyone's humming faltered. The duchess stiffened.

Merely pretty! She was ravishing. The tailor's cousin needed new eyes. My own eyes could barely take her in. Ivi was only a few inches shorter than I, but she was fragile, almost insubstantial. Her honey-colored hair shone as though a bit of sunlight was caught in each strand. Her skin seemed to glow from within, like porcelain. Her bones—in her cheeks, her jaw, her wrists—were more finely shaped than the stem of a crystal goblet.

She and I could have belonged to different species. She was ethereal, and I was base. I'd been a fool to imagine the slightest connection between us.

She advanced in measured steps, as the ceremony required. Her expression was serious. Her gaze was on King Oscaro, except for a peek around the hall. She saw our astonishment and flashed a smile—of triumph, I thought— and then became serious again.

She joined King Oscaro on the stage, and we took our seats.

Sir Uellu, the choirmaster, sang, "King Oscaro!"

The whole wedding would be sung, of course.

"Yes, Ayortha!" King Oscaro's bass voice was full and rich.

Sir Uellu sang, "Maid Ivi!"

Ivi coughed.

The flutist missed another measure.

Ivi whispered, "Yes, Ayortha!"

Several people groaned. Everyone pitied her for losing her voice on her wedding day, but we felt fear as well as pity. This was unlucky. This boded ill. At home in Amonta a sore throat was cause enough to postpone a wedding. But a royal wedding, I supposed, with so many dignitaries attending, couldn't be postponed.

Sir Uellu turned to face us. He sang, "Ayorthaiana!"

We sang, "Yes, Ayortha!"

After that, Sir Uellu sang that this was a marriage of three: King Oscaro, Ivi, and Ayortha. The maiden who married the king also married the kingdom, and the kingdom married her.

Sir Uellu likened king, queen, and country to the Three Tree, which grew only in Ayortha. The Three Tree wasn't one tree, but three: the white obirko, the red almyna, and the black-barked umbru. Their trunks grew no more than an inch apart, and their roots and branches mingled.

Sir Uellu began the "Three Tree Song," also known as the "Song of Ayortha." Everyone joined in.

> "*The wind weaves through you,*
> *My Three Tree.*
> *Your leaves rustle—*
> *Swish,*
> *Whisper,*
> *Sigh.*

> "*Ee ooshahsoo ytyty axa ubensu,*
> *Inyi Uhu Ullovu.*
> *Usaru ovro izhathi—*
> *Esnesse,*
> *Ilhi,*
> *Effosse.*"

I'd sung the "Song of Ayortha" hundreds of times, but never with the king. I wanted to remember everything—the smell of the courtiers' perfume, the king's joy, the bride's beauty (and her whisper), the prince's ears, his dog, the birds trilling, the singing statues.

"The wind whips through you,
   My Three Tree.
   Your branches sway—
   Whoosh!
   Whistle!
   Blow!

"Ee ooshahsoo ukuptu axa ubensu,
   Inyi Uhu Ullovu.
   Usaru yvolky ahrha—
   Ootsikoo!
   Ulhu!
   Iitsikii!"

"My obirko, high and sweet—
   Ayortha!
   My almyna, mellow and light—
   Ayortha!
   My umbru, dark and deep—
   Ayortha!

"Inyi obirko, alara iqui uschu—
   Ayortha!
   Inyi almyna, odgoo iqui ischi
   Ayortha!

> *Inyi umbru, uscuru iqui ascha*
> *Ayortha!"*

The king sang his Wedding Song, declaring the reasons he loved his bride.

> *"She makes me*
> *laugh and cry.*
> *I reflect her glow*
> *and believe that I*
> *am glowing too.*
> *To please her*
> *for a minute*
> *pleases me a week.*
> *She has thunder*
> *and lightning,*
> *rage and joy.*
> *She breathes in*
> *the high notes*
> *and exhales*
> *the low.*
> *She wakes me up*
> *and makes me sing."*

Ivi smiled. She touched her throat and was silent.

◆ ◆ ◆

After the ceremony, the duchess and I joined a receiving line in the corridor outside the Hall of Song. Perhaps fifty people were ahead of us. The line started to move. The duchess stepped forward. I hung back.

"Aza!"

Feeling rising panic, I moved up. I shielded my face with my hand. I hadn't expected to meet the king and the queen and the prince. If I'd known, I'd have thrown myself out of the coach on the way here.

Peeking between my fingers, I saw Prince Ijori, with Oochoo at his feet, greet the guests and announce their names. The duchess and I moved up again. I tried to reason myself out of my fear. Everyone would be polite. The king and queen would be too caught up with each other to pay attention to me. The prince would be too occupied with announcing the guests.

I concentrated on the royal couple and the prince, attempting to prepare myself. The king and queen's love for each other was unmistakable. She leaned into him and clung as tightly as real ivy. He beamed at her and looked prouder than an Ayorthaian lyrebird. As I watched, Ivi's expression turned impish, oh-so-adorably impish. She touched her husband's cheek and whispered in his ear. For a moment he looked discomfited. Then he exploded into laughter, and she looked vastly pleased with herself.

Feeling I was intruding by watching them, I looked instead at the prince, who cocked his head in a doggy way when a guest spoke to him. He traded witticisms with the guests. He seemed to have a light heart and a clever tongue.

When a guest reached the king, he held her hand or put his arm around her shoulder. Ivi whispered, "Thank you," to each one—I couldn't hear, but I could read her lips. She smiled the same smile each time, too, brilliant, but automatic and lacking warmth, nothing like the melting smiles she bestowed on her husband.

I grew desperate. Only a dozen people were ahead of us.

Most guests spoke their congratulations, but some sang a verse of their own composition. One guest had a flawless high soprano. She wasn't as beautiful as the queen, but she was a beauty, dark skinned with a face of gentle curves. She sang,

> "Congratulations!
> May your voices mingle
> Long and late."

The duchess whispered, "We expected the king to marry Lady Arona, who would have been a much better match. And we wouldn't have had such an inauspicious wedding, either, if Arona had been the bride."

Not necessarily. Lady Arona might have had a sore throat, too.

> *"Long and late.*
> *May your double life*
> *Spin a single melody . . ."*

Ivi's smile faded. She smoothed a stray lock of gray hair behind the king's ear. She was demonstrating her claim to him. She was jealous!

> *"Of joy*
> *Forever,*
> *Of joy*
> *Forever,*
> *Of joy*
> *Forever!"*

King Oscaro patted Ivi's hand. Now *I* was jealous. The gesture was so loving. No one would ever pat my hand that way.

He spoke, loud enough for me to hear, "Thank you, Lady Arona. Your good wishes can hardly fail to come true." He paused and then burst out, "Arona, is my Ivi not a wonder?" He turned to Ivi. "My dear, you are always lovely, but tonight you outshine the stars."

Ivi looked smug. Lady Arona seemed to take the king's remarks with good grace. She curtsied and started off, down the corridor.

Four people now separated the duchess and me from the prince.

"Your Grace?" I said.

"Yes?"

"I forgot . . ." What could I have forgotten? "I forgot my handkerchief. I'd better fetch it. I'll—"

"Nonsense. I'm not going to wait—"

"You needn't—"

"How dare you interrupt me!"

Two people remained before us.

"Your Grace, I can't stay. Let me go. I must go."

She understood. "Don't be silly. I didn't bring a companion in order to be alone." She stepped closer to the prince.

I followed her. I was uglier than a hydra. I was as big as the corridor. There was nothing to look at but me.

Prince Ijori announced the duchess. I stood frozen.

She stepped forward. "Congratulations, Sire. Congratulations, Your Majesty. I hope you'll be very happy."

I didn't move. I stared at the floor. My blush was as red as raw meat.

The duchess said, "Aza! The king is waiting!"

CHAPTER SEVEN

I HEARD A GIGGLE behind me. I took a half step forward. Then I froze again. I couldn't do it. I decided to run.

But Oochoo saved me. She came to me, tail wagging madly. I reached down and stroked her long silky ears.

Then Prince Ijori was at my side. He put his hand on my elbow and guided me forward. "Have no fear. The king is dangerous only when he's hungry. What is your name, so I may tell him?"

"A-aza." I had to repeat myself three times before my voice was strong enough to be heard.

I stood two inches taller than the king, hulking over him.

"My dear," he said, taking my hand in his, "if only the ogres were as afraid of me as you are."

He was so kind! I forced out, "Congratulations, Sire."

"Thank you." He passed me along to Ivi.

I curtsied.

She let go of the king and took my hand in both of hers. Her smile seemed genuine now, different from the smiles she'd bestowed on everyone else. "I know how you feel." Her whisper had a Kyrrian accent. She licked her lips. "I was terrified when I arrived here. Petrified! And the wedding ceremony! I'm relieved it's over."

I was thrilled. I struggled and got out, "You're very gracious, Your Majesty. Congratulations." I curtsied without falling over and hurried after the duchess.

The queen had spoken more to me than to anyone else!

It was barely dawn. I heard a peep and then a trill. A lyrebird sang from atop the curtain rod. I heard more birdsong outside my window and from the corridor beyond my door. The birds made for a charming awakening.

We should bring songbirds into the Featherbed. I'd have to tell Father.

I had the morning to myself, and I hoped to explore. The duchess was going to see an old friend. Then we were to attend a centaur performance in the tournament arena. I would see my first centaur.

I looked for a simple gown, but the simplest one had so many ruffles in the skirts that I had to hold my arms out stiffly. Moreover, the matching headdress was a bonnet with a two-foot-long bill.

The corridor outside my chamber was empty, but some-one was singing nearby.

> *"I sing to outwit*
> *the thoughts that come*
> *to mind.*
> *I walk to outwalk*
> *worry. Loss lies far*
> *behind."*

I wondered if the singer might be a corridor troubadour. I hadn't encountered one yet, but the castle was known for them. They were servants whose only duty was to stroll through the hallways, singing. Anything might suggest a song to them: a historical occasion, a boar hunt, even a rainy day.

The corridor ceiling downstairs, on the entry level, was vaulted, twelve feet high at least. Everything was oh so grand, but the stink of the tallow lamps was a whiff of home. Song lyrics, painted in gold leaf and black, covered the corridor walls, each letter as big as my hand. I admired the calligraphy and wished that my brother Ollo, the family artist, could see it.

After more twists and turns than I could keep track of, I smelled baking bread and hot ostumo. My stomach grumbled. I followed my nose.

I expected to hear the same sounds the Featherbed Inn's kitchen produced: plates clattering, pots banging, laughter, an occasional oath. Instead, I heard bells, a harpsichord, and feet pounding in time with the music.

I reached the kitchen—and stood gaping in the doorway. The room was ten times the size of the Featherbed kitchen. In the center was the harpsichord, played by a wench with lightning fingers and a dreamy expression. Activity swirled around her. Serving maids piled muffins and rolls on platters. Three men muscled an ox carcass into a huge oven. A boy peeled a potato that could only have come from a giant's farm. The potato was half as tall as the boy. The pile of peelings came up to his ankles.

The bell ringer was the cook, a red-faced woman almost as big as I was. Her arms were striped with bracelets made of tiny bells strung together with twine. She was cooking in three frying pans at once, cracking eggs into one, flipping pancakes in another, and frying meat patties in a third. As she worked, her arms shook and the bells tinkled. She shuffled from foot to foot in time to her music, shooshing the rushes that were strewn across the wooden floor.

As if a signal had been given, everyone began to sing a morning song.

> *"Climb the day,*
>> *Drop your dreams,*
>> *Possess the day."*

I longed to be part of it.

> *"Uncloak your eyes*
> *And shine the day.*
> *Invoke your voice,*
> *Impress the day."*

I joined in, singing softly.

> *"Stretch and yawn—*
> *Now is the beginning."*

I took a step into the kitchen. A serving maid carrying a stack of dirty plates bumped into me.

> *"Now is the—"*

The dishes went flying. *Crash!*

Silence.

How could I have been so clumsy? The plates were rimmed with gold. They would cost a barrel of yorthys to replace. "I'm sorry. I didn't mean . . ."

Everyone was staring at me. A frozen moment passed. Then everyone was curtsying and bowing. A man with a broom headed my way.

The cook moved her pans off the flame. "What can Frying Pan do for your ladyship?" Her face was expressionless.

I crouched and picked up pieces of broken china. "I'm sorry . . . I should have—"

The woman repeated, "What can Frying Pan do for your ladyship?"

From the floor, I said, "I'm not a ladyship. I'm only an innkeeper's daughter. I thought—"

"Frying Pan thinks the innkeeper's daughter should leave the kitchen." Her voice rose. "Frying Pan thinks the innkeeper's daughter has no business interrupting the king's servants. Frying Pan thinks the innkeeper's daughter should *get out!*"

CHAPTER EIGHT

I STUMBLED BACKWARD through the kitchen door and stood outside, feeling miserable and beginning to be angry. It wasn't a crime for a guest to enter the Featherbed kitchen.

The door opened. The serving maid I'd collided with slipped out. "Mistress—"

"I'm sorry about the dishes. I didn't—"

The maid shook her head, causing the ribbons on her cap to jiggle. "It was my fault. I've been stepping wrong all morning." She was a pretty girl, near my age. I envied her appealing, heart-shaped face.

"Will you or Frying Pan have to pay for the plates?"

"No. Someone breaks something every few— Sweet, that's worrying you? Us, paying for the crockery? You sweet!"

"But then why—" Why had Frying Pan yelled at me?

"Frying Pan would yell at the king if he came into her

kitchen. Are you hungry?"

I admitted I was. The maid, whose name was Isoli, slipped back into the kitchen and returned with two muffins and a russet apple, wrapped in a napkin. Then she went back to her duties. I was sorry to see her go.

I returned to my explorations, nibbling on a muffin. The apple I placed in my pocket to toss away later.

When the second muffin was almost gone, I heard a man singing and people laughing. The entrance to the Hall of Song was a few yards ahead. I believed I was hearing the composing game. My favorite. At home I excelled at it.

I finished eating and stopped in the doorway to listen. Here I wouldn't collide with anyone. Here I wouldn't be noticed.

A courtier was leaving the stage, circling around a mound of books. It *was* the composing game! A dozen people sat in the first row of seats, Prince Ijori among them, Oochoo at his feet.

The dog raised her head and then raced up the aisle to me, tail wagging enthusiastically.

Oh, no! Everyone turned to look.

I put one hand in front of my face, curtsied, and began to leave.

A woman's voice called out, "Wait!"

I stopped. Oochoo put her paws on my chest and tried to lick my face.

The prince exclaimed, "Oochoo, down! Come!"

The dog ran to him. The woman came up the aisle to me. She was Lady Arona, the damsel who'd sung to the king and queen on the receiving line, the one who'd made Ivi jealous. Today she wore a violet gown with a lace fan collar. In place of a bonnet she wore a pearl headband. She looked fetching.

"Providence has come to your rescue, Ijori," she cried gaily. She curtsied to me.

I curtsied, feeling my blush begin.

She said, "The prince has been telling us and telling us that he'd do better with a partner, and here you are." She held out her hand. "Please join our game."

Her face was gleeful. Was she being cruel? Perhaps she thought it amusing to pair the prince with a gargoyle like me.

I wanted to refuse, but I feared what might happen if I did. They were courtiers. I was an innkeeper's daughter. I curtsied again and took her hand.

Prince Ijori, looking disconcerted, said, "Arona! The young lady doesn't want to rescue a hopeless case."

He didn't want to sing with me. I wished I knew what to say to get us both out of it. But I was too shy to speak, even if I'd had the words.

"Rescue a prince?" Lady Arona said. "Of course she does."

Prince Ijori turned up his palms in defeat. "I'll welcome any help she can provide."

Lady Arona started down the aisle, towing me by my hand. My hips and Dame Ethele's skirts couldn't fit in the aisle with her. I followed at an awkward angle.

When I reached the others, they stood to greet me. I wanted to sink through the floor. The prince said, "You're the duchess of Olixo's friend, aren't you?"

He remembered the fool I'd made of myself on the receiving line.

He added, "Lady . . ."

I didn't want to say I wasn't a lady, which would embarrass everyone. But I couldn't say I was. ". . . Aza."

To my horror, Prince Ijori introduced me to everybody. There was a flurry as they curtsied or bowed. I curtsied as he announced each name. The names flew by. There were a count, at least two sirs, several ladies, a baroness, and a duke.

At last, it was over. But then one of the women said, "Where do you hail from, Lady Aza?"

My throat was dry.

They waited.

Trying to help, Prince Ijori said, "Do you live near the duchess?"

If he'd been right, I'd only have had to nod. I shook my head. "Amonta." My voice was a croak.

One of the men said, "That's near Kyrria. Do they even know how to play the composing game there?"

Irritation gave me a bit more voice. "We play often."

Lady Arona said, "Pray tell us your impressions of Ontio Castle."

My impressions? The cook was unfriendly. The nobility were too friendly. The prince was kind. I sent him a look of appeal.

"I see your design, Arona," he said. "You've begun to fear Lady Aza will outdo you, so you want to postpone your turn."

"No such thing. Let the competition continue." She turned my way. "You're next after me. Count Amosa, please . . ."

Next!

The count, a middle-aged man in scarlet hose, picked a thick tome from the pile of books and skimmed through it. "Ah. Here. This part."

I took a seat at the end of the row, a seat away from Prince Ijori. Oochoo sprawled on the floor between us. My heart was racing. Singing was the best part of me. If I could make any sound come from my throat, perhaps I could do well.

Lady Arona took the book and started up to the stage.

Prince Ijori whispered, "She's one of our best composers."

She looked over her selection. "Amosa! I didn't believe you capable of such cruelty."

The books used in the composing game are dense and dull. The referee selects a passage, and the singer must invent a melody on the spot. The singer is allowed to repeat words, but not to change any. When all the players have sung, everyone votes on which tune was best. In the composing game, *best* means silliest, the tune that made everyone laugh the hardest.

Arona began to sing. The tune she came up with was martial and dramatic. She could have been singing about a battle. "The Upuku pig is prone to boils. . . ."

Lady Arona sang stirringly about the many methods of lancing a pig's boil. I laughed along with everyone else. The prince laughed most merrily of all. When she finished, we all waved our hands in the air. She curtsied and left the stage.

I was going to have to stand on the stage. I'd never been on a stage. At home we didn't use one.

Prince Ijori whispered to me, "We'll do respectably. That's the most I ever hope for." He looked rueful. "And the most I ever achieve." Then he smiled.

I was too frightened to smile back. We rose and approached Count Amosa. He marked a page in a book and gave me the book, which I dropped. I bent down for it. The count and Prince Ijori bent down, too. I knocked heads with the count. Prince Ijori picked up the book and passed it to me.

We both mounted the stage, followed by Oochoo. I clutched my book so hard, my fingers hurt. I raised it to hide my face. My book was the second volume of *The Encyclopedia of Sleep*. Prince Ijori had volume one. The procedure for duets is for each player to sing a sentence in turn. Then, at the ends of their passages, they start over, both singing their separate pieces at the same time.

Prince Ijori courteously let me go first. "Show me what I must aspire to."

It's advantageous to be first. The first singer sets the tone. But I couldn't concentrate on the page. The letters seemed to be squiggles.

I squeezed my eyes shut and opened them again. The squiggles formed words.

My passage was harder than Lady Arona's, because it was less tedious. The duller the subject, the easier to inspire laughter. My section contained suggestions for people who have trouble falling asleep, and if some present had that difficulty, they would be genuinely interested. I'd have to struggle against their interest.

I read the passage and tried to think of a single idea.

Count Amosa said, "Highness and Lady, please begin."

Oochoo whined.

I curtsied and looked out over the heads of my audience, too frightened to make a sound.

People shifted in their seats.

I wanted the prince to think well of me, but he wouldn't if my throat was paralyzed. He wouldn't if I lost the game for him.

CHAPTER NINE

MY VOICE FINALLY came—as a squeak. "The following are sixteen—"

The squeak was an accident, but someone—bless him!—chuckled. I repeated "sixteen" on a higher note than even Lady Arona's high soprano had gone.

I dared a glance at the prince and saw he was smiling.

Elated, I sang "sixteen methods for—" I opened my mouth wide in an unmistakable yawn and drew out the next word "—falling . . ." on a falling pitch until I heard laughter.

There!

I repeated "falling," and Oochoo began to howl. I had never sung with a dog before, but I harmonized. I finished my piece that way, with Oochoo's accompaniment, and the laughter almost drowned us out.

It was Prince Ijori's turn. I could face him now that I'd

performed well. He was nervous! I saw it in his expression. I smiled to give him courage, as if I could do such a thing.

He sang, "Some bedframes . . ."

His voice was a beautiful baritone, without a hint of gravel. But his tune was nothing extraordinary, lyrical, not funny. He was witty in speech, but not musically.

Luckily, everyone was still laughing from my performance. I was able to look at them, since their attention was diverted. They regarded him happily, ready to be pleased.

". . . are made of . . ." He hiccuped, a wonderful idea.

Everyone laughed.

". . . hic-hic-hic-hic-hic . . ." He turned to me, and I knew he wasn't sure when to stop.

He could go a while longer. I nodded and kept nodding. He kept going.

I listened to the laughter and noticed when it crested. I stopped nodding and indicated with my eyes that he should move on.

He got it. ". . . hickory, partic-tic-tic . . ." He sneezed—by accident or design—and there were shouts of laughter.

A few more words, and it was my turn again. I borrowed his sneeze and added a new element, a snore.

When we sang together, the hall rang with hiccups and snores and yawns and sneezes. Oochoo stood and barked. It was a triumph. We were a triumph.

Then we were finished. Oochoo stopped barking. I ran off the stage and sank into my seat.

Prince Ijori sat beside me. "We're going to win," he whispered. "I've never won before."

Count Amosa selected a book for the next player.

Prince Ijori added, "But then I never played with Lady Aza before."

Oh! I felt my blush rise again. "Thank you."

"Thank you!"

I smiled and rose. I couldn't stay here, pretending to be a lady. "I must go." I was able to speak without stammering. "The duchess expects me." I curtsied and left.

I felt light-headed and as happy as I'd ever been. *This* was what should happen in royal castles. *This* was a memory I'd have my whole life, singing with a prince, laughing with a prince.

As I turned into the corridor, I heard one of the courtiers say, "Such a voice! It's unfortunate Lady Aza's mother was a hippopotamus."

My happiness evaporated. I heard people laugh. Courtiers could be as cruel as anyone else.

Was the prince laughing too?

I hoped not. I thought not. He wouldn't laugh at someone's expense.

Perhaps my seat would be near his at the Sing tonight. If

he still seemed friendly, I could ask him who won the contest. We could congratulate ourselves if we'd won or commiserate if we hadn't.

If only Dame Ethele's gowns were more becoming. If only they didn't make everything about me look worse!

In the distance the corridor brightened. I hurried toward the light and entered an interior courtyard, which was the hub of my corridor and three others. Benches circled a fountain where water spouted from the mouths of marble singers.

The courtyard was empty. I sat on a bench. If I lived in the castle, I'd come here to escape the people who taunted me.

When I returned home, I'd tell Father we should have a marble fountain at the Featherbed. He'd laugh and laugh. I illused his voice coming from a male statue. "Yes, and a golden chamber pot in every room!"

I illused Areida's voice from a female fountain singer. She changed the subject. "Which do you fancy more," she sang, "the prince or his dog?"

Yarry's bass voice rang out. "No matter. Does the prince fancy you?"

I blushed. Yarry could always make me blush.

Mother's voice came from another statue. "I don't fancy that Frying Pan. We wouldn't keep her."

Mother brought me close to tears, as her sympathy often did. I stopped illusing.

Behind me, someone applauded. My stomach clenched. I didn't want anyone to hear me illuse. Moreover, Ayorthaians never clapped. I turned.

It was the queen!

CHAPTER TEN

*I*VI WAS IN shadow, just beyond a corridor doorway. "I was hoping to see you again. I was wishing for it."

How could that be? I jumped up and curtsied.

She came toward me. "I looked for you at breakfast"— she pouted—"but you weren't there."

Her voice was stronger today. It had a nasal quality that didn't augur well for singing.

"I'd have summoned you, but . . ." Her cheeks reddened.

I wished I could blush so becomingly.

". . . I can't remember your name, Lady . . . Lady?"

"Aza, Your Majesty. I'm not—"

"I'm so glad I found you, Lady Aza." She smiled her dazzling smile.

Footsteps echoed in the corridor she'd come from.

I began again. "I'm not—"

She darted behind the fountain. I followed.

"Lady Aza!" she whispered, looking both frightened and merry. "See who that is. Hurry!"

I circled the fountain and made out the figure of Sir Uellu in the distance.

"It's the choirmaster, Your—"

"Oh, no! He mustn't catch me. Do something!"

I took her hand and ran from the courtyard with her. She ran like a gazelle, and I was hard put to keep up. She tossed her hair and laughed. She turned her head and met my eyes. Her eyes said, Isn't this fun? I couldn't help laughing, too.

We hadn't gone far, however, before her breath gave out. Her pace lagged, and I was pulling her along. I couldn't think what else to do, so I picked her up and carried her.

At first she was rigid in my arms. Then she relaxed and smiled up at me. I felt she admired me, and I relished the feeling.

We reached the end of the corridor. I turned into another and another. I worried we might be going in a circle and would come at the choirmaster from behind.

"This is far enough. You can put me down."

I did so and stood next to her, panting.

"Is he coming?" she whispered. "Did he follow us?"

I listened, but all I heard was my own labored breathing. "We're safe, Your Majesty." Then I blurted out, "Why did we run from him?"

She giggled and slid down the wall until she was sitting on the floor, like a three-year-old. I couldn't loom over royalty, so I crouched next to her. Someone began to sing nearby.

"Is that the choirmaster?"

I'd heard his voice at the wedding. "No."

"Can I confide in you? Will you keep your queen's secrets?"

"Y-yes." I'd never give away a confidence.

"As soon as I saw you last night, I knew I could trust you. I thought, Here's someone who could be my friend. You have such an honest face."

I wondered if she might like me *because* of my ugliness. That had never happened before.

"I'll tell you why we fled. First you should know that my lord told me I had to have singing lessons, because I've never sung in public before."

Her lord? Oh. The king.

She wet her lips. "I don't think I need them, but I don't want to argue with my husband." She dimpled adorably. "Not yet."

I saw her pleasure in saying *husband*. And I was sure her voice was dreadful.

"The choirmaster is to be my teacher. I've been avoiding him all day."

What would she do tomorrow? What would she do when she had to sing? She couldn't have a sore throat forever.

She raised her chin. "My voice is unusual. It's—" She searched for the right word. "—interesting." She nodded, agreeing with herself. "Much more interesting than Lady Arona's voice, which is so admired. One cannot praise Lady Arona's voice highly enough."

She was envious! Beautiful as she was, married to the king as she was, she was emerald green with envy.

I tried to think of something sympathetic to say. The best I could come up with was "The choirmaster *is* imposing. I'd be afraid to speak to him."

"I'm not afraid, and I'll win him over"—her expression turned mischievous—"when I think how. But for now I'm safe." She put her hand lightly on my arm. "You rescued me. You were my salvation."

I blushed. Anyone would have helped her.

"I'd like you to be my lady-in-waiting."

"Pardon me?"

"I'd like you to be my lady-in-waiting. I'm sure you would always be kind."

My heart was hammering. "Don't you have a lady-in-waiting already?"

She grimaced. "Lady Arona. I don't care for her sort of

beauty. She's too soft and floppy looking. Anyway, I don't want her. Oscaro picked her, but I think I should choose my own. After all, you'll be my lady-in-waiting, not his."

"I can't be."

"Why not? Why can't you?" She smiled warmly. "I'm a new queen. You'd be a new lady-in-waiting. We'd be so merry."

I gathered my courage. "I'm a commoner, Your Majesty, an innkeeper's daughter, not a lady."

"*Lady* Aza, I suspect a title can be found for you. I'll speak to my husband. Now will you be my lady-in-waiting?"

I stared at a spot where a green floor tile met a red one just beyond the hem of my gown. If I was her lady-in-waiting, I'd have to live here.

At home they loved me.

"There would be a wage. A generous wage."

A wage!

I could give only one answer. My generous wage would be a godsend to the Featherbed.

Before I could speak, she added, "You have such long thick hair. I can show you how we wear our hair in Kyrria." She licked her lips again. "Some of our fashions would look pretty on you."

I doubted that, but perhaps the different fashions might help a little.

"I'll be honored to be your lady-in-waiting. Thank you, Your Majesty."

"Good. Then it's settled."

As her lady-in-waiting I'd often see Prince Ijori.

She rose. I scrambled up.

"Lady Aza? At the fountain you made voices come from the statues." She looked uneasy. "You did that, didn't you? It wasn't the statues?"

"It was I. I was illusing." I had no reason for concealment. I'd done nothing wrong.

She still looked uneasy. "Can all my subjects illuse?"

"No, Your Majesty. I tried to teach my family, but they couldn't learn. I don't know of anyone else who can do it."

"Oh." She flashed her smile. "How talented you are!" Her voice became peremptory. "I wish to go outside. Conduct me outdoors, Lady Aza. I command it."

How imperious she could be!

I didn't know how to obey. I had no notion where we were or where the castle entrance was. I looked down the corridor, hoping for a ray of sunlight. But in this part of the castle the tallow lamps provided the only light.

Hmm . . . If we exited through a chamber window, we'd be outside. We weren't on an upper story. We wouldn't have to jump.

I bent over and peered through the nearest keyhole, hoping to see an empty chamber, hoping not to see a person in underclothes—or in no clothes at all.

The room seemed to be an office. There were a desk, a chair, a map on the wall. And no occupant.

I opened the door. "Follow me, Your Majesty."

In the room I pulled the curtains aside enough to reveal a narrow casement window, which I cranked open. I stuck my head out. The drop was nothing, no more than a foot. I brought my head back in and put a leg through the window.

The queen looked puzzled, but she'd see in a moment. I gathered my skirts and squeezed them and my other leg outside. The window frame was tight, but I needed only to pop myself through and then I'd be out.

"As soon as I get through, I'll help you. It will be easier for you. You're slimmer." I pushed against the frame, but I was wedged in.

Ivi laughed. She drew the curtains farther aside, revealing a glass door. If I'd even turned my head, I'd have seen it.

What a fool I was! I struggled to get out, but I only locked myself in tighter.

Ivi pushed on my shoulders, to no avail. She could hardly speak for laughing. "I'll find . . . someone . . . to help . . . you. I'll be back shortly." She stepped outside.

I didn't want her to go. I needed help from someone

stronger than she was, but I didn't want to be alone.

What help would she bring? A manservant? Or the king?

Or Prince Ijori?

CHAPTER ELEVEN

I CRANED MY neck and watched the queen until she disappeared around a castle wall. The window opened on a cul-de-sac. I could see only castle walls, a rectangle of grass, a rectangle of gray sky.

The duchess would be expecting me by now. She'd be livid.

Ivi had a good heart. She couldn't be so kind to me if she hadn't. The king couldn't have fallen in love with her otherwise—although he hadn't said a word about her heart in his Wedding Song. I sang a snatch of it.

> *"She has thunder*
> *and lightning,*
> *rage and joy."*

A gust of wind blew into the cul-de-sac. It whipped my skirts up around my waist, exposing my legs. I kicked and wriggled in a useless effort to cover them.

I wanted to scream with frustration.

But then the whole castle would know. I'd be the ugly ox who'd gotten herself stuck in a window with a door inches away.

As time passed, I grew certain the queen had forgotten me. I decided to scream after all. "Help!"

No one came.

I pushed and wriggled again. The window frame bit into my hips, my stomach, and my buttocks. Dame Ethele's reticule jabbed into my right hip.

The reticule! Perhaps I could pull it out and gain an inch or two. I tugged and yanked on its strap. My fingers turned red, but the reticule was as stuck as I was. I was grinding my teeth so hard, my jaw ached.

Then I had to laugh. If I missed a few meals, I'd be able to get out.

I heard the distant roar of a cheering crowd. It had to be the centaur spectacle.

I heard footsteps. I shouted, "Help!"

Perhaps if I twisted diagonally to the window frame, I could pull the reticule through. I twisted, sending pain down my legs.

A man's voice sang, "What's that I hear? A damsel in distress?"

The reticule was out. I'd done it! I squirmed and writhed and gained an inch back into the chamber.

"I'll save you, sweet maiden."

Now that I thought I might get out, I wanted him to go away. I thrust myself forward and gained another inch.

"Perhaps you'll thank me with a kiss."

Go away!

His footsteps were close by. I illused and sent my voice as far as I could, wherever it would go. "Kind sir, hurry please, for I sorely need you."

The footsteps stopped. "Where are you, lovely maiden?"

I sent my voice a different way. "Here I am."

I pushed into the room, progressing inch by inch.

"Where?"

I was free!

"Oh, where?"

He'd see me if I exited into the corridor, so I left through the outside door. I heard cheering again and followed the sound. The clouds were lowering. Rain was on the way.

The lists' stands were filled, although the arena was empty. I supposed the performance was between acts. There was the duchess, looking grumpy and ill-used in a first-row seat. She was facing straight ahead and didn't see me. If she had, she would likely have scolded me before everyone. Luckily, there were no seats near her. I climbed to a back row, ready if she needed assistance.

Spread before me were more colors than in a garden. The stands were draped with cloth—blue cloth here, gold cloth there, green cloth somewhere else. Pennants flew the purple-and-silver Ayorthaian coat of arms. The lords and ladies were gaily clad—the men in their doublets and slashings and brilliant hose, the women in their gowns and ribbons and puffed sleeves.

I saw Prince Ijori and Oochoo, two rows up, with the king and queen. Ivi was laughing and clapping, with no thought for me, trapped in a window. But perhaps she had sent a servant to save me, and the servant had been derelict.

The arena was set up with hurdles, too high for ordinary horses. Centaurs streamed in, six stallions and six mares. The muscles of their horse bodies flowed into their human torsos and arms. The tight doublets of the stallions and the clinging bodices of the mares concealed none of the creatures' strength and grace.

A mare stood directly below my part of the stands. Her eyes had the questioning look of an intelligent dog, and she sniffed the air with her human-seeming nose.

The centaur trainer entered the lists, carrying a basket and a baton. He held something up for King Oscaro and Ivi to see. Then he displayed it to the rest of the audience—an egg. He threw it to the mare near me and reached into his basket for more.

Each centaur received four eggs. The trainer waved his baton, and they began both to juggle and to gallop. When they reached a hurdle, they jumped while still juggling. I smiled.

I glanced across the lists. Prince Ijori was smiling too. Our eyes met. His smile widened and my blush started.

I looked at the king and queen and caught a little drama. King Oscaro had turned his head toward Lady Arona, who was enchanting in a pink embroidered bonnet. Ivi's eyes followed his gaze. The fury in her face frightened me. I wouldn't have been Lady Arona then for anything.

A moment later the queen laughed, and I wondered if I'd imagined her rage.

The centaurs started lobbing eggs to one another, sometimes halfway across the lists. I could barely breathe, expecting one of them to miss and an egg to land *splat*. Not a single egg was dropped. I raised my arms until my shoulders ached.

Frying Pan entered the arena, wheeling a charcoal brazier and carrying a bowl and a skillet. The trainer took the bowl while Frying Pan lit the charcoal. The centaurs trotted to the trainer. Each one cracked his or her eggs into the bowl and galloped out of the lists, followed by the trainer.

Frying Pan placed her frying pan atop the brazier. Everyone laughed as she beat the eggs and poured them into the pan. She sang,

> *"Shake an egg*
> *Toss an egg*
> *Catch an egg*
> *Break an egg*
> *Omelette for lunch!*
>
> *"Watch it bubble*
> *Watch it boil*
> *Watch it burn*
> *Watch it scorch*
> *Omelette for lunch!*
>
> *"Please, oh cook*
> *Quick, oh cook*
> *Cook, oh cook*
> *Serve, oh cook*
> *Omelette for lunch!"*

Frying Pan lifted her pan off the flame. "Omelette for lunch!" She wheeled the brazier out of the arena.

The overcast sky darkened.

The centaurs trotted back in. The trainer returned, too, pulling nets filled with pulsing color. He opened the nets and released swarms of butterflies, which settled on the centaurs.

The centaurs turned into creatures out of a dream, garbed in bright hues that shifted and throbbed as the butterflies fluttered their wings. The centaurs began to move, slowly and carefully. The butterflies stayed with them!

The centaurs had completed a circuit of the lists when they began to trot. And the butterflies stayed with them. How could it be? But it was.

The centaurs cantered and then they galloped. They raced out of the arena with the butterflies still clinging. I hated to see them go. There might be more miracles ahead, but I could have watched this one forever.

There was a lull. Servants circulated with omelette sandwiches. Mine was the best I'd ever tasted, studded with sweet peas and mellow eland cheese.

After we'd eaten, four huge centaurs entered the lists and strutted about, showing off their bulging muscles.

I felt a raindrop on my nose. Servants opened umbrellas over the heads of the courtiers. An ox entered the arena, pulling a cart filled with wooden posts and heavy iron rings. Mud spattered the cart's wheels.

At first the rain didn't matter. A servant hammered four

wooden posts into the ground in a line. Then he drove the cart to the centaurs. With great difficulty he lifted out an iron ring and staggered with it to a mare.

She lifted the ring as though it were paper. With a flick of her wrist, she tossed the ring onto the farthest post, almost the length of the lists away.

The rain came down harder. Each centaur took a half dozen rings. At the trainer's signal, the centaurs hurled rings at all the posts, faster than I believed possible. Not a single ring missed its post.

The centaurs started to trot while tossing the rings, their aim still perfect.

King Oscaro stood and shouted something. The trainer signaled with his baton, and the centaurs increased their pace. A stallion slipped in the mud while tossing a ring. He recovered, but his throw went wide. An iron ring hurtled toward Ivi.

King Oscaro moved to block her. Prince Ijori launched himself at her and knocked her over.

The moment is lodged in my memory. If they had done nothing, the ring would have sailed over her shoulder. Instead, it smashed into the side of King Oscaro's head.

CHAPTER TWELVE

THE KING TOPPLED onto Prince Ijori and the queen.

A cry rose from the lists. Everyone clambered down and rushed toward the king. I don't know what we hoped to do.

I thought, The bad luck has arrived. This happened because Ivi didn't sing at her wedding.

She squirmed out from under King Oscaro and Prince Ijori. Then the three of them were hidden by the crowd. The trainer herded the centaurs out. I stood in the arena, on the edge of the throng.

Ivi shrieked, "My lord! Oscaro! Prince, make him answer me. I command you. Make him stand up."

I heard Prince Ijori's voice. "The king lives!"

I think we all breathed again. Ahead of me the crowd parted. I stood aside as Count Amosa and Prince Ijori came through, carrying King Oscaro. Tears streamed down Prince Ijori's face.

I had my first clear view of the injured king. His head was bloody. His face was as white as mine. His body hung limply between his two bearers.

"Where are you taking him?" Ivi cried.

"To the physician," Count Amosa said.

They began to carry the king out of the lists. Oochoo loped alongside, her tail down.

Ivi saw me. "Lady Aza! Come to me!"

It didn't matter if she'd forgotten me in the window. I went to her, and she threw herself into my arms, weeping. "What will happen to me if he dies?"

This was what she was thinking? I patted her back and murmured, "Don't cry. It's all right. He won't die." I was talking as much to myself as to her. "He'll be fine."

With the queen clinging to me, I followed Prince Ijori and the count.

Ivi wailed, "Don't leave me alone, Oscaro. Who will love me now?"

I heard someone gasp. I was shocked. She wasn't crying because she loved the king, but because he loved her.

The physician's chambers opened onto the same cul-de-sac where I'd been trapped. Those who couldn't fit into the examining room stood on the grass outside.

Since I was with the queen, I was allowed in. The duchess gained entry too. I saw her astonishment when she noticed me.

Sir Enole, the physician, came out of his study. He rushed to help Prince Ijori and the count. They laid King Oscaro on the couch. Prince Ijori straightened up and saw me supporting the queen. For a moment he looked surprised. Then I saw him forget me as Sir Enole felt for a pulse in the king's neck.

Ivi surged away from me. She grasped the physician's robe. "Make him well. Make him talk to me."

"Your Majesty—" Sir Enole drew his robe out of her hands and bowed. "I will do my best."

Ivi came back to lean against me. I put my arm around her waist.

Sir Enole examined King Oscaro's wound. The bleeding had stopped, but the area was puffy. "First we must bring that swollen flesh down." He turned away.

Ivi shrilled, "Where are you going?"

"To my stor—"

"Will he live?"

"His pulse is weak but steady. He will not soon die."

I found myself smiling and crying at once. The physician's words spread through the room and to those waiting outside. People laughed and hugged one another and repeated, "He will not soon die."

Ivi said, "When will he speak to me?"

"I do not know." The physician's voice was choked with tears. "He may speak in a week or never again." He headed toward a storage cabinet, then stopped. He knelt and swore his loyalty to Ivi.

She was our ruler now! Everyone in the room and those outside knelt and swore their loyalty. I knelt, too, and she swayed against my shoulder.

How could she rule? She didn't know Ayortha. How frightened and grief stricken I'd be in her place.

Sir Enole spread an unguent across the king's wound. Ivi told me she wanted to go to her chambers. She leaned on me as we started for the door. Prince Ijori placed himself on her other side, and she took his arm.

The duchess looked put out.

I bobbed a curtsy to her. As we went by, I whispered, "I'll come to you as soon as I may." I couldn't suppress a feeling of triumph. The queen wanted her lady-in-waiting.

I hoped I could comfort her.

The songbirds above us trilled as merrily as ever. Oochoo stayed at my side through the corridors. We made slow progress. Ivi moved as haltingly as an invalid.

She moaned, "Ijori, cancel tonight's Sing. No one will want it now."

No! She mustn't cancel the Sing!

He said, "Your Majesty, we want it more than ever."

She sank to her knees on the corridor tiles and looked up at us, her eyes enormous.

Oochoo stood nearby, wagging her tail.

"You can sing when my Oscaro's so ill?"

Prince Ijori said, "It will be a Healing Sing. Our songs will help him recover."

I forced myself to speak. "At Sings we write our own songs. Your song will contrib—"

"I have to write a song?"

"You don't *have* to," Prince Ijori said, "but everyone will want to hear your words."

To encourage her to participate, I said, "My songs are simple and not very good."

Prince Ijori said, "Canceling the Sing will make the king sicker."

I nodded. It was what we believed.

She wet her lips. "I must rest. I need my rest. And I must grieve. Now help me up. I'll decide about the Sing while I rest."

At the door to her chambers, she said, "Ijori . . . Prince . . . I will count on you in the coming days." She reached out and touched his cheek.

He drew back. I doubted my eyes. It had been such an intimate gesture.

"Aza, bring me a cup of ostumo in an hour." She smiled bravely. "Your good Ayorthaian ostumo will fortify me for what lies ahead."

◆ ◆ ◆

When I left the queen, I hurried to the duchess. In her room I apologized for seeming to desert her, and I explained that the queen was making me her lady-in-waiting.

"How can she make you a lady-in-waiting when you're not a lady to begin with?"

I blushed. "She is making me a lady as well, Your Grace."

"Why not make you a countess and have done with it?" She strode to her wardrobe and selected a gown. She held it out to me. No, *at* me. It was a challenge. She wanted to see if I'd dress her, now that I was on the threshold of nobility.

I did, and I was docile as could be.

The queen called out that I might enter.

I opened her door and stopped on the threshold, dazzled. The floor of her chamber was spread with rugs, so many that they overlapped. The walls were hung with tapestries of hunting scenes, garden scenes, mountain landscapes. The brocade curtains were patterned with an autumnal forest. The ceiling was adorned with a pastoral fresco. The curtains were drawn. The room was dim, lit by oil lamps in golden sconces.

Ivi sat in an easy chair at the fireplace, her feet on a tufted ottoman. A few yards away was another door, which, I later learned, led to the king's bedchamber.

She stretched and rolled her shoulders, reminding me of Imilli. "I would do anything to save my lord." She took the ostumo. "You may have your Healing Sing, provided . . ." She drank.

Provided what?

". . . provided that you illuse for me."

Gladly! I made the silver pitcher on her washstand sing in a metallic voice. "I will illuse for you day and night." I made the pottery Three Tree on the mantel sing,

"Inyi umbru, uscuru iqui ascha—
Ayortha!"

She smiled. "No. I want you to illuse for me tonight."

My hands felt icy. I wondered if I was understanding her.

"Illuse a voice that seems to come from my lips. Give me the kind of voice people here love, a beautiful Ayorthaian voice."

I couldn't! She didn't know what she was asking.

"I've wished for such a voice. I've longed for it ever since Oscaro asked me to be his bride. I've tried spells, but—"

"I can't! I'd be deceiving everyone."

She rose and carried the ostumo to her dressing table. In addition to the usual mirror above the table, a hand mirror lay on its surface, amid a myriad of creams and powders and rouges and, of all things, a golden flute. She put the mirror in the table drawer. "I want the choirmaster to know I have a beautiful voice. I want everyone to hear my voice."

But it would be my voice. "I can't. I mustn't." I should have lied and said I wasn't capable of it, my illusing wasn't good enough.

But the lie never occurred to me, and I was certainly capable of doing what she wanted.

"Everyone else has a beautiful voice." She sat at the dressing table. A stool had been placed close by. "Sit by me. Lady Aza, I want my subjects to love my voice. Oh, please, illuse for me."

I sat. "If I illuse for you, your song won't help the king, and the deception may harm him." It might be better not to have the Sing at all.

"There will be many more songs than mine and many other singers." She wet her lips. "My Oscaro will surely be healed by all of them. If my voice wasn't pretty—for an Ayorthaian—mightn't it harm him?"

Did she really believe in the power of singing? I wondered if she wet her lips before a lie.

"You're his wife," I said. "Your song will be the most important one. It won't help him unless you sing it."

She shrugged. "We have no Healing Sings in Kyrria,

yet people recover from their injuries. Aza, sing for me. It won't harm my lord. It will harm no one. It will only help your queen, your benefactress."

"I can't, Your Majesty. I'm sorry. I mustn't."

"You must!" She leaned closer to me until her face was only an inch away. I smelled the ostumo on her breath. "Aza, Aza, Aza. Don't you see? If you won't illuse for me, then you're not my friend." She pushed back her chair and stood. "Your friendship isn't worth a pin. And if you're not my friend, then I don't want you to be my lady-in-waiting."

I'd return home, where they cared about me.

But there would be no generous wage.

And no prince.

"If you're not my friend, you're my enemy and an enemy of the kingdom. The proper place for an enemy of the kingdom is a prison cell."

The room seemed to tilt.

"I don't think your inn should flourish, either. I think its license should be revoked."

I gripped the sides of my stool—I was sure I'd fall if I didn't.

She took my face in her hands. Her Kyrrian accent was heavier now. "But I want you for a friend. I don't want to do those dire things."

She didn't let go. I belonged to her. She could throw me in prison. She could harm everyone I loved.

I didn't want to be imprisoned. I couldn't let her hurt my family and the Featherbed.

"I'll illuse for you."

CHAPTER THIRTEEN

S HE STILL HELD my face. "Not only tonight. For as long as I need."

I was terrified. "I know." She'd need me often.

"Oh, thank you!" She released my face and spun around in raptures. "You'll sing for me! You won't regret it. My lord will get well. You and I will be friends forever. Secrets make friends of people."

I wondered if she was mad.

"Aza, you must tell no one. No one. Anyone you tell will be my enemy too and will suffer as much as you."

"I won't speak of it." I wished I could run from her presence and never stop running.

She flew to her desk across the room. "Here is my song." She gave it to me and returned to her ostumo.

She'd known before I came in that she could make me do what she wanted.

"It's a letter," she said. "A letter is all right, isn't it? Oscaro told me songs don't have to rhyme."

"A letter is acceptable. We frequently sing epistolary songs."

Her song was short. The beginning was bad and the ending was worse. The beginning sounded just like her. The ending might have been written by someone else. The song would sit well with no one.

"What do you think?"

I didn't care if she made a fool of herself.

"I must be a powerful queen. Don't you agree?" She watched me closely.

Let everyone hear the song. Let them hate her almost as much as I did.

But the terrible words might also hurt the king.

I said, "Perhaps you can revise it a bit. Songs in a Healing Sing are supposed to be about the sick person, but the last part isn't about King Oscaro."

"I tell him not to worry! That's about him, isn't it?"

"Yes, but—"

"Go on. We're friends." She hugged me. "You can tell me anything."

"Your song," I said, concealing my revulsion, "shouldn't mention Kyrria or what you're wearing." That was only the beginning of what was wrong.

"Oscaro loves my gowns! He'd want to know what I chose for his Sing." Her face saddened. "I miss my lord. I wonder if he misses me." She closed her eyes and sighed.

My heart went out to the king. It would be a miracle if the Sing helped him.

She dismissed me with instructions to tell Prince Ijori the Sing could go on. "Send him to me. He can tell me how to make you my lady-in-waiting."

First he'd have to be told I wasn't a lady. He'd think ill of me. I should never have pretended.

That had been my first deception. Illusing would be incomparably worse.

I found him at the entrance to the Great Hall, stroking Oochoo's head and looking out at the Three Tree. When he turned, I saw he'd been weeping again. I said that the Sing was to take place.

"Lady Aza!" His voice was so pleased that my blush threatened to melt my face away.

"But her song is all wrong."

"How?"

I told him.

He shook his head. "She doesn't know our ways. Perhaps I can help her change the words."

I hoped he could!

"How did you persuade her to hold the Sing at all?"

I'd never been a convincing liar, but I had to be one now. The fabrication came easily, evoked by need. "I thought she might be worried about rhyming, so I assured her that her song didn't have to rhyme. Then I suggested she write an epistolary song, and she thought she could."

"You have as much magic as a fairy. You cast a spell over the queen. And before, you contrived for me to win at the composing game."

Me? Magical? "We won?"

"We won. Lady Aza, I'd never come close before."

I took a deep breath. "Er . . . I'm not a lady." I told him who I really was.

His face reddened. "You lied?"

A lump rose in my throat. "Everyone thought— I was embarrassed. I should have said."

"It doesn't matter." His voice was unfriendly.

He hated me!

I saw him shrug off his anger. "My uncle—" He stopped speaking. "My uncle"—he sounded really miserable—"just married a commoner." He smiled wanly at me. "I don't mind that you're one too."

I forced myself to tell the rest—the rest that I *could* tell. I didn't want him to hear it first from Ivi. "Queen Ivi wants you to make me a lady. That's why she's summoned you. She wants me to be her lady-in-waiting."

His steps slowed. "How did you accomplish that? In such a short time, too. You do have magic!"

This time it was not a compliment.

After I left Prince Ijori, I went to the duchess and helped her with her toilette for the Sing. When she was dressed and combed and bejeweled, I left her.

In my room I chose my gown. This one's bodice was striped brownish red and purplish brown. The overskirt was covered with huge squares of the same colors. The headdress was a purplish-brown band atop which stood a wooden bird.

I illused a mournful chirp coming from the top of my head.

Now I had to write my song, although my brain was reeling and my feelings were a muddle of fear and fury and sadness. I concentrated on the king.

Surprisingly, the first three lines came quickly.

> *In Amonta, at the Featherbed Inn,*
> *Where I once lived, my mother*
> *Rakes up the fire.*

Mother and Father and my brothers and Areida would be distraught when they learned of the king's accident. They revered King Oscaro. The first course of every meal in the tavern was served in his honor.

But their distress would almost be overcome by delight over my elevation to lady-in-waiting. If they knew how the queen was treating me—

That way lay tears.

I wondered if the king's condition might have improved— or worsened. I wondered if he was comfortable, if he was chilled, if he could hear the people around him, if he could think.

I hoped the tainted Sing wouldn't harm him.

A line came, and then another. Here is my song:

> *In Amonta, at the Featherbed Inn,*
> *Where I once lived, my mother*
> *Rakes up the fire.*
> *My father wakes the cook,*
> *Who cannot cook today.*
> *Cream curdles; milk sours;*
> *Eggs break; onions rot.*
> *My father and mother*
> *Put down their forks.*

In his castle, the king
Swallows nought but air.
His life has narrowed,
But his thread winds on.

Should the king come to Amonta,
Eyes wide, legs hale,
Mouth full of words . . .
Cakes would bake themselves,
Mares shoe themselves, roads
Pave themselves. My mother
Would don her damask gown.
And I would sing
Until the sun cheered
And the inn dissolved
In music.

The queen answered my knock in a sleepy voice. When I stepped inside, her eyes were closed, her face unguarded, and she appeared hardly more than ten years old. She sat up and watched me draw her bath, as if she really was a child. Her expression showed no consciousness of what she'd done to me.

While she soaked, I sat at the dressing table to memorize her song and put a melody to it. It was the same song I'd seen before. Apparently Prince Ijori had had no more success than I in persuading her to change it.

I picked the golden flute up from the table and turned it over idly in my hand. As I considered the tune and reviewed the words, I blew into the flute. No sound came out. I set it down. It was merely a decoration.

When I thought I knew the song, I looked away from the page to test myself. The hand mirror was back on the table. In turning aside, I happened to look into it.

My reflection began to change. My chalky skin darkened a tone to alabaster. My cheeks turned a pearly pink. My rage-red lips softened to the hue of a ripe strawberry. My pulpy cheeks gained definition. My sooty hair became lustrous. Even my absurd bird headdress looked charming.

Only my eyes were unchanged. I was stunningly beautiful, beautiful beyond any hope I'd ever had.

CHAPTER FOURTEEN

I LOOKED AT LEAST as beautiful as Ivi, though in a different way, grander, not so delicate. Strangest of all, despite being greatly altered, I was somehow still myself.

I touched my face, but I couldn't feel any difference. Could I really have become beautiful? I raised my head to the mirror above the dressing table, and there was my ugly face. I looked into the hand mirror. Beautiful again. I turned the hand mirror over, seeking a clue to the mystery. Carved into the wood was the word *Skulni*.

Ivi called out for a towel. I looked into the hand mirror—Skulni—again. Now I saw nothing. No reflection, only glassy gray. How could that be? Then Skulni clarified. I saw my usual reflection.

"Oh, Lady Aza, where's my towel?"

I fetched the towel. What had I seen? I gave Ivi my arm to lean on as she stepped out of the tub. Had I imagined the reflection? I helped her into her satin shift, which buttoned in the back. I began to button it but had to stop because my hands were trembling.

She laughed. "I'd hoped for a *speedy* lady-in-waiting."

"I'm sorry, Your Majesty." I took a breath, and my hands steadied.

So that was how I'd look if I was beautiful.

When she was dressed, in a coral-colored gown with embroidered sleeve liners, she sat at the dressing table while I brushed her hair.

"Did you learn the song?"

"Yes, Your Majesty." I sang the melody. "Would you mouth the words?"

She sat on the bed and did so. I accompanied her softly, although I could hardly keep my mind on the song. My beautified face floated before me. A magic mirror! Did it produce only illusions, or might its magic alchemize me from lead into gold?

I pity anyone who's never experienced an Ayorthaian Sing. Participants in a Sing, especially a Healing Sing, are wrapped in an embrace of fellow feeling, neighborliness, kinship, love. Yes, love. The embrace was particularly loving tonight, because the sick one was our adored king.

But I felt apart from the embrace, because of the role

I was about to play.

Prince Ijori sat next to me, with Ivi on his other side. I felt his disapproval of me, although he said nothing. Oochoo put her head in my lap. I patted her with a trembling hand.

Singers perform in reverse order, according to their rank. Ivi was slated to sing last. I wasn't her lady-in-waiting yet, and as an unknown commoner, I was to sing first.

People were still settling into their seats. Silk and satin rustled. I heard whispered greetings.

Sir Uellu raised his gold baton. We all began to hum. He nodded at me. I stood and took a step—and my slipper heel caught on the hem of my underskirt. I stumbled and would have fallen, except that Prince Ijori saved me.

His hand was on my elbow, and his arm was around my waist. I almost fainted.

He lurched, because of my weight, no doubt. He caught himself, and when we were steady again, he released me. I mounted the steps to the stage, praying to remain upright.

Laughter rippled through the crowd. They were laughing at me, at my stumble or my ensemble or simply my person. I looked down to hide my blush and saw the true reason for the laughter. Oochoo had followed me up to the stage and was sitting at my side, apparently ready to sing.

My first note was a mumble. I couldn't get enough air to sing.

I heard a low whistle. Oochoo raised her head, then trotted down from the stage. I found my breath and began.

By the third line, everyone was silent, listening. By the beginning of the second stanza, many were holding hands and swaying. The duchess was swaying but not holding anyone's hand. She wasn't a hand holder.

My melody was intricate, but I hoped it wasn't daunting. I wanted Amonta to sound idyllic and remind people of their home villages. I wanted my song to reach the king and remind him of his loving subjects beyond Ontio. That might strengthen him.

> *"And the inn dissolved*
> *In music."*

I finished with a tricky trill. Most of the hands in the hall went up. Prince Ijori's hands were up, and he was smiling. Even Frying Pan near the door raised hers.

Ivi's hands were up, but her expression was angry. She was jealous of my voice! Jealous, even though she needed my voice for her voice.

I left the stage. The next singer took my place. I reviewed Ivi's song and discovered that I couldn't remember one of the sentences. A complete sentence! Ivi would have to leave it out. But how could I tell her, here in the middle of the Sing?

The missing sentence returned to me. Everyone would hate it. I reviewed the song again. And again.

Eventually I came out of my fright and heard the remaining songs. Some were adapted healing incantations from Ayortha's primitive past. Some were remembrances of the king. Some were exhortations to him to rise and defeat his injury.

My favorite was the physician's. This is a bit of it:

> *"In dreams, friends float to me.*
> *They murmur. Make me well.*
> *Don't let me die. I mumble*
> *Incantations. Get well.*
> *Do not die.*

> *"Oh, king,*
> *You float to me.*
> *Your face is granite.*
> *I raise you above the water.*
> *I push you below. I acquaint*
> *You with the tides. Do not die."*

My second favorite was the choirmaster's. Sir Uellu sang that he'd been unable to sing when he heard the news. Now his voice cracked twice. The cracking, unintended and heartfelt, only added to the beauty of his song.

After the choirmaster it was Prince Ijori's turn. I smiled encouragingly at him, as if my encouragement would matter.

This was how he began:

> *"My lord, are you in pain?*
> *Uncle, are you in pain?"*

I wept. It was hard to bear, to think of the king in pain. He ended with:

> *"I wish my head had borne*
> *The blow that felled a king."*

Oh! I didn't wish that. I wished no one had been hurt.

After Prince Ijori's song, Princess Elainee sang. Ivi was next. My throat was closing.

Someone would catch us. I'd never mislead them all.

When the princess finished singing, Ivi rose. She didn't seem frightened. She'd do her part perfectly, but I'd fail. We'd both be disgraced. I'd go to prison.

My throat was dry. I swallowed, but no saliva came. I couldn't sing with a dust-dry throat.

She held her arms at her sides, palms out, as the other

singers had done. She threw back her head and opened her mouth.

I came in on time. I gave her Mother's voice, bell-like and clear as mountain air. It was as delicate as Ivi herself, with unexpected reserves of force and air.

Sir Uellu dropped his baton.

> "Dear Oscaro, I miss you dreadfully,
>   more dreadfully even than your head must hurt."

I stayed with her on every word. She caught my eye and smiled as she sang. I blushed.

Several people swayed and nodded. Sir Uellu picked up his baton. I sensed his ears almost vibrating with the intensity of his listening. I didn't let my voice waver—or my mouth move—but my jaw felt like ice.

> "I have not yet stopped weeping. I hope my
>   singing pleases you. I am arrayed in a yellow gown,
>   yellow for sadness."

The swaying slowed. The words were what a child might write.

> "If I look well, it is for you. The gown's

> *pretty train stands for my grief, which drags*
> *behind me wherever I go. I will rule*
> *Ayortha for you, so you must not worry.*
> *I will be a powerful queen."*

Fewer and fewer people swayed or nodded. She began the part that didn't sound like her.

> *"I shall expect obedience, loyalty, and*
> *respect from my subjects."*

I saw people exchange looks. She was no longer singing about the king, and nothing in her words would help him get better.

> *"The hallmarks of my rule will be a firm*
> *hand and a stern heart. I will rely on the*
> *governing principles of my native Kyrria."*

At the mention of Kyrria I felt the mood in the hall turn angry.

> *"They say this Sing will make you better. I*
> *will make Ayortha better as well. I live*
> *for your awakening."*

My gaze happened to fall on Frying Pan, who looked like a pot about to boil over. A few people dared to stamp their feet.

Ivi smiled her most dazzling smile. She must have felt everyone's response. I would have run off the stage, but she continued to mouth words. I sang the ending.

> *"Your affectionate wife and ruler of Ayortha,*
> *Queen Ivi."*

She held out her arms, as though receiving a tribute. She turned from side to side, including everyone. Then she left the stage, not hurrying, still smiling.

CHAPTER FIFTEEN

PRINCE IJORI AND I followed Ivi out of the Hall of
Song. As soon as the door closed behind us, she stopped
smiling. She stormed through the corridor.

"They should have loved my song. They shouldn't have
hated it. I said I miss Oscaro."

The prince and I hurried to keep up. Oochoo trotted
between us. My shadow and the shadows of Prince Ijori
and Oochoo merged into a shapeless splotch on the corridor
wall. Ivi's shadow, thin and wavery, bobbed ahead.

"I said my grief trails—"

Prince Ijori broke in. "Your Majesty, perhaps—"

She whirled on him. "Why did you let me say the wrong
things?" She whirled on me. "Why did you?"

I said nothing. I'd seen guests in rages at the Featherbed.
The only sensible course was to wait out the fury.

He said, "But Your Majesty, if you—"

"Don't contradict me!"

We marched on. After a few minutes we reached Ivi's door. Oochoo sat, wagging her tail.

"You needn't come in. Aza, I think I remember how to disrobe."

I curtsied and Prince Ijori bowed. Ivi went inside, slamming the door behind her.

We left her chambers, a dispirited trio. Even Oochoo's tail was down.

We heard a crash. She'd thrown something. I hoped it hadn't been Skulni, the hand mirror. Oochoo ran away, down the corridor. A moment later we heard Ivi weeping. I couldn't pity her. We hurried after Oochoo.

When we were far from her door, Prince Ijori said, "I trust you'll be silent about the queen's outburst."

"Of course."

We reached the Great Hall. It was dim, illuminated by only a few lanterns. Our heels echoed on the tiles. Prince Ijori guided me to a table where a candle burned. On the table were several unlit candles in candleholders.

He lit a candle for me. "Can you find your room from here?"

"I think so." I wished I could have news of the king before I tried to sleep. "Do you think your uncle's condition might have changed?"

"I was intending to visit him. You may come if you like."

It was a grudging invitation, but I wanted to go with him and learn whether the Sing had harmed or helped.

He took a candle for himself. We entered a new corridor.

When he spoke again, his voice was strained. "Tomorrow I'll draw up the papers to make you a lady and the queen's lady-in-waiting. You cannot join the nobility unless your family owns land. The queen is graciously giving you a parcel of the crown's land, fifty acres. It is excellent—"

"Pardon me." I stopped walking. My knees felt weak. "Did you say land? Your Highness, did you say fifty acres?"

He waited for me. His voice was a shade friendlier. "Yes, and your wage will be ten gold yorthys a month."

I touched the wall to steady myself. Ten gold yorthys a month! Fifty acres! This would mean everything to the Featherbed, to my brothers' and Areida's futures. I murmured, "We're rich!"

"There's also a gallon of rendered boar fat on the first day of winter." His face was in shadow, but his tone was amused. "The fat is customary."

Ivi was paying me well for my crime. I began to walk again.

He added, "My uncle chose Lady Arona to be the queen's lady-in-waiting. Arona knows the ways of the court."

And I knew nothing.

I wanted to promise him that I'd serve the queen faithfully, but I didn't know what faithful service to her would mean. I wanted to promise I'd serve Ayortha faithfully, but I was engaged in duping the entire court. After a moment I said, "I'll do my best to serve her honorably." I would try to do that. I would try to serve her well in spite of herself, in spite of my fear, in spite of my anger, in spite of my duplicity.

"I hope you will. I hope you'll serve Ayortha honorably, too."

I think my heart stopped beating for a full minute. I heard Oochoo's panting.

He changed the subject. "Your song comforted me."

Without thinking, I said, "Yours made me weep." At home that was a compliment. Was it a terrible thing to say here?

"I saw. Thank you. But your song— It was a comfort to know that your family, so far away, would feel as keenly for my uncle as we do here."

"We love the king at the Featherbed. Father collects reports of him from our guests. Every year, in honor of his birthday, Mother and Father and my brothers and my sister and I write a song to celebrate."

"I'd like to hear you all."

If only he could! "We'd give you the Peacock chamber,

where the duchess stays." It would seem shabby, compared to the rooms here.

"What would your cook serve?"

"Hart with fire peppers." I sang,

> *"Peppers in the pan*
> *Make your mouth dance.*
> *Peppers on the tongue*
> *Make your nose run."*

Then I blushed. At least it was too dark for him to see. He laughed, really laughed. Oochoo jumped up on him. He sang,

> *"Peppers on the tongue*
> *Make your nose run."*

I wanted to sing him every silly song of my childhood. I was pleased at taking him out of his sadness for a bit.

As we turned into a new hallway, he said, "Perhaps the queen chose well in choosing you. She may prefer a companion to an instructor. My uncle would understand that."

I whispered, "Thank you, Your Highness."

"When she blamed us for her song, I argued with her. Did you wish to argue too?"

I shook my head. "When guests rage, it's best to let the rage blow itself out."

"Were they always terrible, your guests who raged?"

How nice, to be royalty. No one had ever before dared to behave badly to him. "Some were decent and good, once they stopped being angry."

We reached Sir Enole's chambers.

Prince Ijori put his hand on the knob but didn't turn it. "If we're to attend the queen together, you should call me Ijori."

Ijori? Ijori! I didn't think I could say it, so I nodded.

He patted Oochoo. "Oochoo answers to 'her royal high-houndyness.' Shall we go in, Aza?"

"Yes, please, Prince Ijori."

"Ijori."

"I can't."

"You can. Yes, please . . ."

"Yes, please . . ." My voice dropped to a mumble. "I-ijori."

CHAPTER SIXTEEN

THE MAIDSERVANT WHO'D stayed at the king's side during the Sing said that he'd been agitated while it took place.

"His breathing is easier now," Sir Enole said. "The Sing may have helped him. It's too soon to tell."

Ijori pulled a chair next to his uncle. I stood just inside the door, knowing I didn't belong. I was nothing to King Oscaro, only a subject. The king's hand was curled at his side. His cuticles were bitten ragged. I had no right to see that. I curtsied and left.

In my room I couldn't sleep. Behind my closed eyelids, faces kept floating into view—Ivi's, Ijori's, the king's, and my own, made beautiful in Skulni. I was awake half the night, and in the morning I was tired and homesick.

I sang another childhood ditty:

> "I'm solitary as a pulled tooth,
>   Lonely as an unwelcome truth,
>   Lost as a minnow out of school,
>   A genius in a crop of fools."

I penned a letter to my parents, telling them what had befallen the king. Then I wrote,

> You will scarcely credit what has happened.
> The queen has made me her lady-in-waiting. I
> cannot explain it . . .

Or I'd go to prison.

> . . . but it's true. There is to be a wage and land,
> and I am to be a lady."

I told them the particulars, struggling for a happy tone and hoping my words didn't seem forced. I ended by asking them to kiss Imilli, the originator of my good fortune.

Although I wanted to tell them about Ijori, there was little to tell. He was handsome and charming and good-natured. He loved his dog and distrusted me.

When I dressed for the day, I picked among Dame Ethele's remaining ensembles, all overdecorated, all loathsome. The one I selected was patterned in brick red and purple and green and pale blue.

Why couldn't Dame Ethele have liked just one color?

I left my room and went to help the duchess with her packing. She was surprisingly cordial and promised to deliver my letter. She even said I could keep Dame Ethele's gowns as long as I needed them.

On second thought, that may not have been cordiality. It may have been punishment!

After I managed to lock the duchess's bulging trunks, I bade her farewell. She was my last tie to home, and soon she'd be gone. She was bad-tempered and difficult, but she meant me no harm, and I'd miss her.

In the Banquet Hall I asked a serving maid for a tray I could take to the queen.

Wondering what my reception would be, I knocked on the door to Ivi's apartments. There was no answer. I knocked again, and again received no answer.

"Lady Aza!" Ivi hurried down the corridor toward me, her robe billowing out behind her. The sun streamed through the corridor windows, bathing her in light. She was a celestial creature.

"I was in the physician's sickroom with my lord, with my Oscaro." She flowed onto the bed and lay, looking up at me.

I wondered if she was telling the truth. "How does the king fare?"

"He passed a peaceful night." She sat up and positioned herself to accept the breakfast tray on her legs.

I placed it and poured ostumo into her mug from the linen-wrapped silver urn. I scanned the room for Skulni. There it was on the dressing table, unharmed. I went to the table on the pretext of straightening her jumble of perfumes and creams. I saw only my ordinary reflection.

Shards of porcelain littered the hearthstone. I swept them up with a whisk broom.

"Thank you, Lady Aza." She wet her lips. "I had a clumsy accident last night. So clumsy of me. Thank you for my breakfast and for my voice last evening." She smiled up at me. "I beg your forgiveness. You gave me a voice beyond compare, and in return I blamed you for my song. It was unforgivable, yet I hope you'll forgive me." She waited for me to speak.

"There's nothing to forgive." I sounded stiff and angry, so I made myself smile.

She put down her cup. "My dear, have you been to the tailor yet?"

"W-what? Er, I beg your pardon, Your Majesty."

She laughed. "As my lady-in-waiting you'll need a new wardrobe."

A new wardrobe hadn't occurred to me. It would be heavenly—if the price hadn't been my honesty.

"We can go to the tailor together." Her face was eager. "Oh, Aza! It will be such fun! I'm a connoisseur of fashion. My taste is impeccable."

I didn't want her to accompany me to the tailor, and I certainly didn't want her there when the seamstress measured me.

She moved the tray off her legs and bounced out of bed. "I wish I could hold a ball, as we do in Kyrria. You'd wear a new gown, and so would I."

She began to dance with an invisible partner. Step, step, glide. Glide, glide, dip. She tilted her head and smiled coquettishly.

She stopped. "I was going to ask Oscaro for a ball. Now I can't. I miss him, Aza. I miss my lord." She went to the window and looked out.

I straightened her counterpane.

"Aza . . . do you think the prince has the look of a king? Is he regal enough?"

"I-I don't know." My temples were pounding.

She was still looking out the window. "Those ears. Those absurd ears. I wish I could find a fairy to shrink them." She laughed. "But he has more hair than Oscaro, and my subjects know him, and he is a prince already."

She was choosing her second husband, the king's successor!

She faced me. "Your eyes are as big as melons, Aza. More than anyone, I hope my lord will live. He loves me, so of course I want him to live. But I have an advisor, who also loves me, and this advisor tells me that, if the king does not live, I must marry again, for the good of Ayortha."

Who was her advisor?

She giggled. "And for my own good, I'd like my husband to have nice ears."

My own ears were hot enough to start a fire.

On our way to the Great Hall, we passed the serving maid Isoli, who was carrying a tray. She was the maid who'd knocked into me in the kitchen. When she was out of earshot, Ivi said, "How pretty the wench was. Did you think her pretty?"

I said I did. I wished I was half so pretty.

"Did you notice her complexion? Was it as clear as my own?"

"I don't know, Your Majesty."

"Oh? You think her complexion might be as fine as mine?" Her voice was dangerous.

I began to worry for Isoli. Ivi's claws came out with no warning. Acting the fawning flatterer, I said, "Hers must not be as fine, because yours is perfect."

"You are a dear."

We continued down the corridor. I found pity mixing with my fear of Ivi. Yes, she was ruthless, but she was also fretful and discordant. How did she endure herself?

I had a fright before we reached the tailor. Sir Uellu saw us enter the Great Hall and approached. I wanted to run and hide. The sight of him made me feel like the greatest criminal in Ayortha.

He bowed to us, which made me feel worse. I curtsied. The queen inclined her head.

He inquired into our health. Ivi answered that we were in good health and were bolstering our spirits by selecting my new wardrobe.

He nodded absently, then said, "Your Majesty, you and Lady Aza have uncommonly fine voices. I should love to hear you sing a duet."

A duet! I couldn't!

Ivi smiled graciously. "We will prepare something for you."

I'd have to tell her I couldn't illuse a duet. It wasn't possible.

I was so shaken, I heard nothing else the choirmaster said, although he and Ivi chatted for several minutes. Then he took his leave, and we continued to the tailor.

He and his four seamstresses were set up near a tall win-dow that provided good light for their work. Their stall was bustling. A woman was being fitted for a gown. Another was sketching a design with a seamstress. Several more were going through bolts of fabric.

The tailor bowed to Ivi, then to me. I raised my hand to block my face.

Ivi said, "My dear friend Lady Aza is in need of six gowns, underclothes, three sleeping costumes, and a cloak—all in the finest fabrics."

How could I afford so many things?

"Lady Aza is to be garbed as a maiden of rank."

At that, the women in the booth stared at me. I wanted to be elsewhere, anywhere—in the branches of a tree, in a cave, stuck in a window.

"Spare no expense. The crown will pay."

I stammered out my thanks as everyone watched.

The tailor made a show of looking me over. "I cannot help your friend if she wishes this sort of apparel." He ges-tured at my gown.

"No!" I said. "Not this sort."

"Then perhaps we can do something." He called to one of the seamstresses, who led me behind a screen to undress and be measured.

To my great relief, Ivi didn't follow us. The seamstress,

Mistress Audra, was pleasant. "This must be such a treat for Milady," she said, "picking out your wardrobe. The gown you are wearing now was not of your choosing, yes?"

"Yes!" I said fervently.

"My goodness! You are as tall as our screen." She unrolled her tape measure.

I had to crouch for her to measure the length of my neck. She said nothing, but she exclaimed, "Ayortha!" when she measured its circumference.

I flinched.

When she measured the distance from my neck to my shoulder, she said, "Prodigious!" Then she sang, loud enough for half the Hall to hear, "Milady, you are vast."

CHAPTER SEVENTEEN

MISTRESS AUDRA CONTINUED measuring. After several minutes she burst out, "Lady Aza, it is not very interesting to be a seamstress, and then someone like you—"

I hummed in my mind to drown her out, but I heard her anyway.

"I measure you, and being a seamstress is fascinating. How will we subdue those hips? How will we narrow that tree-trunk waist? How will we—"

Ivi poked her head around the screen. "I must run to a meeting of the king's council." She made pouty lips. "It will be tedious, I'm sure." She brightened. "But I've left fabrics for you to consider."

"Thank you, Your Majesty."

"Oh, it's nothing. I can't wait to see you in your new things." She left.

"So terrible, what befell the king," Mistress Audra said. "I once measured him for a doublet. King Oscaro has a big heart in a narrow chest. You are finished, Milady. I'll wait outside."

I dressed and emerged from behind the screen.

Mistress Audra was at the fabrics table. "Come, Milady. See the fine fabrics Queen Ivi has selected for you."

I liked everything she'd chosen. Each fabric was rich, but none was gaudy. My favorite was a midnight-blue brocade with a ribbon design in an almost imperceptibly lighter shade of blue. I also loved a violet silk so smooth that touching it felt like touching water.

I spent a while longer with Mistress Audra, going over patterns. I picked the simplest fashions in gowns and headdresses, until she complained. "Milady, this is boring. No lace or bows on your head, no puffed sleeves or trains in your gown. People will look at you and go to sleep."

Sleep would be an improvement over the usual reaction, but I agreed to let Mistress Audra add a few embellishments.

"Very modest. Very discreet. I understand. Milady prefers to make an understatement."

"Mistress Audra, will the new gowns . . ." I hesitated. "Will they make any difference?"

"My sweet lady, they will make all the difference. You are

shy. You do not like to jump out at people. I am right, no?"

I nodded.

"Your new gowns will look like the finest gowns of the other nobles. Your form will be improved, and you will not be so much noticed."

The tailor said the gowns wouldn't be ready for six weeks. However, my four copper yorthys persuaded him to hurry. My fitting could take place in twenty-nine days. I'd have my gowns the day after that, right before the next Sing.

When I left the tailor, I started for the entrance and fresh air. But my steps slowed. I could put my free time to better use by visiting the library, where I might learn something of magic mirrors or the meaning of the word *Skulni*. I found a manservant to lead me there.

Inside, the birdsong paused and then took up again. Perhaps birds could read, because there seemed to be at least as many in the library as in the rest of the castle. And birds' nests! The top shelf of every bookcase had a nest, and some of the lower shelves did, too. Frying Pan could find enough eggs here to feed the entire court.

Even so, there were more books than birds. I had never seen so many. I wondered if the king spent much time here. I wondered if he liked books. I wondered if he would ever read again.

Bookcases blocked the windows. I walked through

the aisles and squinted at a book title: *Tooth, Tongue, and Trilling*. I pulled out the book and opened it. On the recto was an illustration of a portion of the tongue and several teeth. The vantage point was of a tiny person, standing on a huge expanse of tongue ringed by a wall of towering teeth.

The verso was dense with words. I read a sentence: "Tooth preservation must be the primary object of the conscientious singer."

I replaced the book and read a title across the aisle: *The Singer's Hiss*. A bookcase in the next aisle was filled with time-of-day songbooks. The opposite bookcase held nothing but songbooks about food and eating: *Muffin Songs*, *Soup Songs*, *Songs to Chew On*, and the like.

Areida would revel in the songbooks. She adored old songs and odd songs, and she remembered every word after a single hearing.

I looked at another title: *Maudlin Ostumo Love Songs*. Marvelous!

But so far I hadn't seen anything about magic or mirrors. I wondered if this was the songs-and-singing library and if there was a second library for other works.

No. The shelves in the next aisle were full of volumes about Ayorthaian history.

In the aisle after that, I discovered I wasn't alone.

At the end of the aisle a man slumped over a desk, his

head resting on his forearms, his tangled gray hair spilling to one side. I backed away quietly. He was probably the library keeper. If I woke him, he might direct me to a book about magic mirrors.

But he'd know exactly why a blemish like me wanted it.

I decided to look awhile longer on my own.

In the next aisle I spotted a book called *Court Life: Habits, Rules, and Manners*. Not spells, but something else I could use. I opened it to the index and found—

> Lady-in-waiting, 7, 89, 248–251
>> compensation to, 251
>> duties of, 249–250
>> in household hierarchy, 27
>> origins of, 7, 34
>> privileges, 250
>> selection of, 248

I turned to page 249, but just as I found it, I heard the scraping sound of a chair being pushed back. I returned the book to its shelf. A hoarse but tuneful voice sang,

> "Is Anyone Here?
> *A book of lonesome songs.*
> Is Anyone Here?

A good title, not overused.
Is Anyone Here?
Aisle twelve, second shelf west.
Is Anyone Here?
Just next to Where Were You?
Is Anyone Here?
I'm truly asking,
Is anyone here?"

"I'm here," I sang without leaving my aisle. Maybe he could help me without seeing me. "I'm looking for a book about magic mirrors."

He limped into my aisle, a stoop-shouldered man with one leg shorter than the other. He said, "You have a fine voice, Milady, the finest I've heard, reminds me of—" He sang:

"Queen Amba, Voice of Ayortha,
A noisy title, but not overused,
Aisle four, center, top.
She hated ostumo, so they say
Great-granddaughter to an ogre,
Or so they say.

"Not a full book about magic mirrors." He sang, "*Magic Artichoke Pitters and Other Curious Objects*, a good title—"

❦ 131

He broke off and said, "I'll show you. It's with the spell books."

He limped down the aisle and led me to the shelves across from the blocked west window. He peered at the shelves, and I did, too. I read, *Try This! Strange Enchantments*, and *No Harm Done: Safe and Simple Spells*. The binding was falling off *New Spells for New Times*.

Perhaps one of them contained a beauty spell.

"Ah." The book was on the top shelf, under a nest. He supported the nest with one hand while he pulled the book out.

"Let me see." He thumbed through it. "It's alphabetical. *M* . . . Ah, here."

He sang, "'Magic mirror: Unique. Little known about. Commanded by maverick fairy Lucinda and often dispensed by her as a wedding gift.'" He switched to speech. "You'd be surprised how often that Lucinda pops up in these magic books. I hope she never pops up in person, by the sound of her." He sang again. "'Mirror has beautifying and other appearance-altering properties in conjunction with magic potions.'"

Beauty potions?

"'The creature within the mirror is called Skulni, a creature of unspecified abilities.'"

Ivi had that very mirror!

"'He may always alter whomever he reflects, but he may show himself and may speak only to those who've drunk one of the potions.'"

That's why I was beautiful in the mirror. He'd made me beautiful, to please me or to taunt me.

The library keeper read on. "'He may escape under certain unspecified circumstances. The mirror may be destroyed under certain unspecified circumstances.'" He closed the book. "The tome might have another title." He sang with disgust, "It should be called *Unspecified*, not overused."

The most astonishing thought came to me: The mirror— or the potions, or Skulni—may have made Ivi beautiful. She might once have been plain. She might have been as hideous as I was now.

Probably not hideous, if she'd received the mirror just before the wedding. The king wouldn't have fallen in love with a hideous maiden. I recalled what our Amonta tailor's Kyrrian cousin had said of her, that she was "merely pretty."

I heard the library door open.

A female voice said, "Master Library Keeper?"

"A good title," he said. "It belongs to me, but I didn't make it up."

The newcomer was a maidservant, seeking—me! The

queen wanted me. I felt frightened.

As we left, I heard the library keeper sing,

> "Don't Go! More Songs to Keep You—
> *A good title, not overused.*
> Don't Go! More Songs to Keep You,
> *A songbook in—*"

The door closed behind us. I would return when I could. I wanted to look at the beauty spells.

CHAPTER EIGHTEEN

*I*VI WANTED me to accompany her on a visit to the king.
As we approached the physician's chambers, we heard a
lute and Sir Enole singing a sickroom song.

> *"Cook up the soup!*
> *Rich meat for strength,*
> *Hot broth for fever,*
> *And spices to chase*
> *The sickness away.*
>
> *"Make up the room!*
> *Silk sheets for ease,*
> *Blankets for snuggling,*
> *And fire to burn*
> *The sickness away.*

"Bring in the people!
Father for comfort,
Mother for cuddling,
And good friends to laugh
The sickness away."

When we entered, a servant set aside a steaming bowl and bowed. The king seemed unchanged from last night, except that his cheeks were stubbly with a day's growth of beard. A bead of porridge stood on his chin.

That gob of porridge pained me. He was our king!

The servant used her handkerchief to wipe off the porridge.

Ivi knelt by her husband, weeping. She turned to the physician. "Has he spoken my name?"

Sir Enole put down his lute and bowed. "I'm sorry. He has said nothing."

"Is he at all improved?" I asked.

Sir Enole just looked sad. The servant held the bowl of porridge, waiting to finish feeding the king.

I started for the window. I wasn't looking down, and I almost fell over a pallet on the floor.

Sir Enole said, "Your Majesty, I had a softer mattress brought in and a warmer blanket. If you stay again tonight,

I hope you'll be more comfortable."

"My lord," Ivi said to the king's slack face, "I am here with Lady Aza." She took the chair the servant had vacated. "This morning I helped Lady Aza choose her new wardrobe. The tailor has excellent goods." She described fabrics and patterns, omitting not a single detail.

The servant put down the porridge, curtsied, and left. Sir Enole began to roll bandages. I stood at the window. My mind wandered to beauty spells.

"At the council session . . ."

I came alert.

". . . all they talked of were droughts and trade delegations and ogres. It was too dull to endure. They said the same things over and over."

She rested her forehead on the king's chest. "So I dissolved the council."

Sir Enole's hands stopped their work. I choked back a gasp.

"I don't see why I need a council. Ijori can tell me what I must decide."

Dissolved the king's council!

Ayorthaians were proud of their council, the oldest in our region. There were only five members, including the king or queen, but one member always had to be a commoner. We'd fought a civil war to put a commoner on the council.

Council matters were discussed all across the kingdom.

"My lord, you will thank me when you are well." She recited, "'Powerful monarchs need no parliaments.' I wonder you—"

This was tyranny! I burst out, "Your Majesty, everyone will be furious. The king's council—"

"Oh, Aza, leave statecraft to your queen. Leave it to me. You are not to worry." She gestured for me to approach her. I did, and she whispered in my ear, "My advisor assures me that it will come right."

Obviously offended at her rudeness, Sir Enole retreated to his study.

She added, reciting again, "'Powerful queens rule happy kingdoms.'"

I returned to the window, half wanting to assassinate her for the good of Ayortha.

She told her husband the dishes she hoped would be served at dinner.

Later, on my way to my chamber after Ivi had bade me leave her for the night, I saw Ijori and Oochoo in the Great Hall. He was tossing a wooden ball, and she was dashing among the pillars in hot pursuit. When I happened along, she rushed to me, tail wagging, ball in her mouth. She let me have it, and I skimmed it across the tiles.

He approached. "I hoped you'd come. The moon is out. You haven't seen Ontio Castle by moonlight."

I followed him outside, amazed he'd waited for me, amazed he wanted to show me anything. He seemed unaffected by my ugliness, but it gnawed at me. At least at night I was less visible.

We passed under the leaves of the Three Tree and across the courtyard. I breathed in the scent of obirko blossoms.

He started down a steep stone stairway. "Hold on to my shoulders. I don't want you to fall."

Joy. I grasped his shoulders. He felt sturdy under my hands. I heard Oochoo, scrabbling down the slope on our right.

The steps ended in a pebbled path, almost as steep as the stairs.

"Careful. This is treacherous at night."

I didn't see why. Every pebble stood out under the bright full moon. The path leveled, and the moat opened up before us. The water was low. I saw a fox's footprints on the banks.

Ijori stopped and turned. "Look up."

I did, and there was the castle. If the earth tilted a degree, it would come crashing down.

He sang, "What do you think?"

The glossy leaves of the castle's ivy caught the moonlight. I sang, "It glows." I wanted to add something memorable, something to rival the castle's grandeur. "It's . . . It's enormous. It blocks out half the sky." Not memorable.

"It's indescribable, although I've tried innumerable times."

I felt better and found the words I'd wanted. "It makes me think of the sound when a chorus sings full voice."

"Ah. Yes."

We began to walk again. A cloud crossed the moon. Ijori stood still, and I did too. The world was dark. All I had were the warmth of him next to me and the noises of the night—Oochoo panting, frogs chanting, a breeze in the bushes.

The cloud passed. We went on.

"We can circle the castle along the moat."

"Where are the swans?" I asked.

"Asleep."

We walked in silence. I thought if I concentrated, I might hear the stars serenading each other.

He said, "Do you hear Oochoo?"

"Not anymore."

"Where is she?" He called, "Oochoo, come."

Silence.

He whistled and called again. In the distance we heard her. A minute later she was jumping up on Ijori and then nuzzling into my skirts.

"Good, Oochoo. Good, girl." He fed her a treat from his

pocket. "Stay with me." For a moment he held her by her jeweled collar. "She won't stay. She never does."

He let her go, and she ran off again.

"I never thought to have a friend like you." He resumed walking.

He and I were friends? "I never thought to have a prince for a friend."

"Princes are cut from good cloth for friendship. Silk is as strong as burlap, although no one thinks so."

"I think so."

"Thank you, Aza." He paused. "I have a cousin who's a friend, but she's entirely different."

What did he mean?

"It's because I'm a commoner. You can put a *lady* before my name, but at bottom I'm burlap."

"You're not burlap," he said gallantly.

I chuckled. "We do have a bit of dimity here and there at the Featherbed."

"Now I have a confession. The shocking truth is I've never spent a night at an inn."

"Never? Then how do you travel?"

"From castle to castle. Or, if I'm riding against ogres with Uncle, we sleep in tents."

Riding against ogres. Terrifying.

"An ogress almost killed me when I was fourteen."

"Oh!"

"She persuaded me that my father was alive. I knew he was dead, and yet she convinced me in only a few words. I believed she could lead me to him. Uncle saved me." He laughed. "For a moment I was furious with him."

"How did he save you?"

"He was on his charger, singing so loud he couldn't hear the ogress, and he snatched me up." He shook his head. "Sometimes in nightmares I still hear her sweet voice, and I still believe her. Ogres are the ultimate deceivers."

I ranked just below them.

I heard voices in the distance. People were singing in the garden.

"Aza . . . If I may ask, I'd like your opinion of Her Majesty—the opinion of an innkeeper."

I didn't know what to say. I didn't know what *his* opinion was. I searched for something safe. "She's inexperienced."

"I shudder to think what she'll do when she has experience. How could she have dissolved the council?"

"She doesn't understand what it means to us."

"How could she not—" He stopped himself. "I'm being indiscreet." He sang, "You must despise me." He whistled for Oochoo again, and this time she came quickly.

"No. I don't." He was confiding in me, but I was hiding everything from him.

"You're too kind to despise anyone."

Such a compliment! I despised Ivi.

Not entirely. Sometimes I had sympathy for her.

How I wished to unburden myself! How I wished to be frank!

He added, "I'm candid because I need someone to assess my judgments. You and I know her better than anyone here, excepting my uncle."

I was uneasy even about sharing my complete opinion of her. "She's headstrong, and we know she has a temper, but it's perhaps because she's so lively."

"Yes. My uncle loved—loves—her liveliness. He said her moods made him feel young again. He said she made him think he could do anything."

"I believe she returns his love." I told Ijori that she'd spent the night at the king's side.

He was surprised and pleased.

"She's generous, too." I told him she'd paid for my wardrobe.

This failed to impress him. "The crown is rich enough for such generosity"—he touched my arm—"but I suspect you'd find goodness in an ogre."

"I detest ogres! I detested certain guests at the Featherbed."

"What did they do?"

"Oh . . . they were rude."

"Rude?" He paused. I could feel his thoughts go round. "I see."

He probably did. I wished he didn't.

"Which guest did you like best?"

I told him about the gnome zhamM. "And I like the duchess of Olixo."

"That's tantamount to liking an ogre."

"It isn't! She loves cats."

"And ogres eat them. I see the difference."

I laughed.

He circled back to Ivi. "At least she spent last night at the king's side."

"Yes."

"And at least she has a first-rate voice."

CHAPTER NINETEEN

A WEEK PASSED. THE mood in the castle was bleak. The corridor troubadours sang of pain and grief. Whenever I illused for Ivi, I was sure the word *trickster* would appear on my forehead. I feared sneezing or hiccuping or fainting. I felt dizzy and feverish.

At the beginning of the following week, I received two letters, one from home and one from Areida at finishing school. I opened them in my chamber before dressing for dinner, sitting at my window, reading by the light of the sunset.

Areida's letter contained mostly questions, paragraph after paragraph of questions about the royal family, the court, and the castle. Then she wrote:

> *Since I received Mother's letter with your news, I've fallen asleep happy and awakened smiling. I knew eventually someone would truly*

see you. It took a stranger—a queen with clear
eyes and extraordinary common sense. Perhaps
these abilities are why the king loves her, because
she recognizes quality when she encounters it.

Darling Areida. I was glad she didn't know the truth. I patted her letter and smoothed out its creases. I put it aside and turned to the letter from home, which had been penned by Mother, the family chronicler. First came the family's distress over the king, then her joy over the change in all our fortunes. I basked in her excitement. Because of our wondrous wealth, a new roof had been decided upon and a new wing was under consideration.

She wrote,

The duchess is not fond of the queen, but then
the queen isn't a cat. We, on the other hand,
cannot stop singing her praises! Please convey
our feelings if you think it proper. I have no
notion what's proper to convey to a queen!

Evidently word of the council's dissolution hadn't yet reached home.

The tone of her letter altered.

*Daughter, your father insists I tell you this.
We've kept it secret for fear you'd become dis-
contented with your lot. But now you're where
you belong, and you should know the truth:
The courtiers are your equals.*

    *We are convinced you were highborn. You
may even be a king's daughter. The blankets
we found you in were velvet, hemmed with
gold thread.*

I had to catch my breath. I looked out the window, where
the green of the oak leaves and the brown of the branches
were saturated with dusk. The colors swam, and I realized
I was weeping.

The woman who'd borne me and the man who'd sired
me had been rich enough to keep me if they'd liked, but
they'd wanted nothing to do with me. They hadn't even
made sure I lived.

I wondered if Areida and my brothers knew of my high
birth. Probably not. They wouldn't have been able to keep
the secret.

I wiped my eyes and read on.

    *We believe you are a child of Ayortha
because of your voice, but we may be wrong.*

You could have come from anywhere, from Kyrria or Bizidel or faraway Pu.

If people snub you, remember you may belong higher above the salt than they do. You weathered snubs at home, and see where you are now. Father and I are proud of you, as we've always been.

I'd had more luck in my adoption than I'd had in my birth. No king or queen could have been kinder than an innkeeper and his wife had been. They'd taken me in, an ugly baby and an added expense. Yet I hadn't been merely a charity. They'd loved me.

I put the letters in the top drawer of my bureau and dressed in yet another of Dame Ethele's horrors. This one had so much draped cloth in the sleeves that they would have been useful on a sailing ship. The headdress, too, was cursed with excess cloth, which culminated in flaps that fell on each side of my face like the long droopy ears of an Ayorthaian hare.

Ivi's gown was as different from mine as ornamental cabbage is from a rose. The cut was simplicity itself—a round neckline and a gently flaring skirt. Eighteen tiny silver buttons ran from neck to hem, and the cloth was deep purple silk embroidered in silver thread with tiny fleurs-de-lis.

As I buttoned the eighteen buttons, she said, "I fear the prince may not be speaking to me at dinner." She stood. "He's vexed because I won't send anything south."

There was a drought in southern Ayortha, and the peasants needed food and supplies desperately.

"Their lords can help them," she added. "I will not deplete my husband's coffers just because of the weather."

I thought even Ivi would sympathize with starving peasants, and I thought the king's coffers were meant to be used for droughts and floods and the like.

She looked around. "Where is my brooch?"

We couldn't find it, although we looked under everything and behind everything and rifled her drawers twice over. I didn't care if she found the brooch or not, but I had my eye out for vials that might hold potions.

No vials, and no brooch.

In the end she found it, an amethyst-and-jade pin, on the dressing table, in the shadow of the golden flute, next to Skulni. I pinned it on and returned to what was important. "The drought—"

"You are not my advisor."

I was her lark.

"Aza, I am acting on good counsel."

I decided she was corresponding with a friend in Kyrria, who knew nothing of us. Still, only an enemy of Ayortha would recommend ignoring a drought.

I opened the door and we stepped into the corridor. A guard fell in beside each of us as we began to walk. I'd never been so close to swordsmen before. They wore breastplates and helmets, and their swords clinked with each step. For a moment I thought they were going to escort me to prison.

"Why are the guards here?" I asked.

"A powerful queen should look powerful. She should seem mighty. And people may have heard my decision about the drought."

No Ayorthaian ruler had ever before needed protection from her own subjects.

Before dinner was served, I illused her part in the Song of Ayortha. Tonight, as was often the case, Sir Uellu's eyes rested frequently on me. I ached to know what his sharp ears were detecting. I was particularly nervous during the choral portions. I couldn't sing at full strength for both of us. I gave most of my voice to Ivi, reserving just enough for myself to keep my neighbors from wondering.

When we finished, he said, "Your Majesty, the court has been waiting for your duet with Lady Aza. If you perform together at the coming Sing, you'll have two weeks to prepare. Give us the pleasure of hearing your voices mingle."

I thought my heart was going to fly out of my mouth. I had explained to Ivi that I couldn't illuse a duet. She'd told me not to worry—she was queen and Sir Uellu was merely a subject. But he wasn't. She had no idea of his importance.

She wet her lips. "Perhaps we will."

Dinner was brought in with unusual ceremony, each plate concealed under a domed silver cover. When all had been set down, serving maids and scullery maids and even Frying Pan herself stationed themselves between the diners. Frying Pan's bracelets jingled lightly.

Ivi clapped her hands. "A surprise!" She smiled around the table. "What do you think it might be?"

At a signal from Frying Pan, the covers were removed with a flourish. Everyone's plate was piled with glistening roast hare, barley, mushrooms, onion pie. Everyone's plate except Ivi's, Ijori's, and mine. We each had a mound of leavings—potato peel, picked-over bones, bread crusts, eggshells, fruit rinds.

I gasped.

Ivi shrieked.

Lady Arona laughed.

Ivi rose. Her chair fell over behind her.

What would Ivi do to Frying Pan and anyone else

involved, and to Lady Arona for laughing?

Ijori laughed too, as if at a prank. He was so quick-witted! I joined in and made my laughter hearty. Lady Arona's laughter had been genuine. I could tell Ijori's was forced. A singer would know the difference, but Ivi might not.

The courtiers understood and laughed too. The servants began to laugh. As we made ourselves laugh, true mirth flowed in. Frying Pan had done something defiant and dangerous, and we were turning it into a jest to save her and Lady Arona.

Frying Pan looked startled. Then she laughed too, belly bellowed with laughter, her cheeks shaking, her bracelets chiming. Lady Arona sobered and then laughed again, her eyes on Ijori. She knew how clever he'd been.

Ivi finally laughed too, but her laughter was uncertain.

When the glee subsided, Ijori said to his server, "Enough merriment. Bring our dinner."

A serving maid picked up Ivi's chair. She sat. Our plates were whisked away and proper ones brought back from the kitchen. A more relaxed dinner followed than any since the wedding. Conversation was easier. Songs were sung between courses, and five or six were sung after dessert. We were all giddy from relief.

As we ate, I considered each older courtier, seeking

resemblances to myself. This one had a pale complexion. That one had fat cheeks. This one was oversize. None looked much like me, but any one was possible.

Were any hard-hearted enough to forsake a babe? I couldn't tell.

That night I couldn't sleep. Mother and Father thought I belonged in the castle, but—except for Ijori—I would a thousand times rather have been at the Featherbed. Here I was essential to the queen's misrule. I was an instrument of every step she took. I thought of running away, but her vengeance on Mother and Father would be swift, and she'd send her guards after me.

If only the king were well. If he were, I'd throw myself on his mercy. I didn't think he'd send me to prison.

Since I couldn't sleep, I would put my wakefulness to use. I'd had no daytime opportunity to return to the library, but I could go now.

I dressed hurriedly, lit a candle, and took a spare, plenty to last until dawn.

As I traversed the halls, my excitement mounted. If I found a potion recipe or a spell, my every moment would be transformed along with my appearance. Eating would be transformed, because I'd no longer picture my broad cheeks stuffed with food. Walking down a corridor would be transformed, because I'd no longer feel my lumbering gait. Dressing would be transformed, because every ensemble would become me.

After my metamorphosis, I'd tell Ijori what I'd done, and I'd face down everyone else. I'd faced people down over my ugliness all my life. It would be easy to face them down over my beauty.

Except Ivi. I didn't know what she'd do to me.

But I wouldn't be frightened out of taking this chance. She could hardly imprison me. I couldn't sing for her from a dungeon.

In the library the birds were asleep, except for a talkative whippoorwill. I went directly to the shelves that held the spells and pulled out a book called *Secret Spells for Secret Uses*. I sang, "A good title, but I don't know if it's overused."

I made room for my candle on a shelf at eye level. The book had an entire chapter of beauty potions and spells! I turned to it and discovered why more than one spell or potion was needed—and why everyone in the castle wasn't beautiful. The first spell had to be chanted when three comets were in the sky at the same time. The second was written in a runic language I couldn't read. The first potion recipe required an ogre's bloody knuckle! The second called for the fur of a six-legged cat.

I remembered a book I'd seen before, *No Harm Done:*

Safe and Simple Spells. That seemed the book for me.

I used up half the first candle to find it. When I finally had it, my trembling hands made turning the pages difficult. It had no potions, but the table of contents referred me to three beauty spells, on pages 138, 187, and 363. The first spell could be done, but it involved boiling a long list of ingredients. I didn't think Frying Pan would like me preparing a spell in her kitchen.

The spell on page 187 needed only to be sung. The words were in a language I didn't know, but the letters were Ayorthaian. I hoped it wouldn't matter if I botched the pronunciation here and there. The spell was merely a single stanza, repeated thrice.

The instructions were to start loud and finish soft. They promised the effect would be immediate.

I smoothed out my skirts and patted down my hair, as though making myself presentable to the spell. I wanted to remember the date, May the twenty-third. I was fifteen, but this would be my true beginning.

I sang, loud as I could.

> *"Hyong weeoon, chia eeung layah*
> *Chia eeung layah; ix ayunong*
> *Layah ix ayun ong moiee*
> *Ayun ong moiee eviang tuah.*

Moiee eviang tuah preeing: ang
Tuah preeing ang, ang hyong."

I stopped reading. The words came as if I'd memorized them. I didn't sing softer deliberately. The spell was taking over.

"Hyong weeoon, chia eeung layah
Chia eeung layah; ix ayunong
Layah ix ayun ong moiee
Ayun ong moiee eviang tuah.
Moiee eviang tuah preeing: ang
Tuah preeing ang, ang hyong."

My singing was reduced to a mutter. I could barely move my jaws.

"Hyong weeoon, chia eeung layah
Chia eeung layah; ix ayunong
Layah ix ayun ong moiee
Ayun ong moiee eviang tuah."

I took a breath, although I almost couldn't make my chest expand. But I had to finish the spell.

"Moiee eviang tuah preeing: ang
Tuah preeing ang, ang hyong."

Was I beautiful?

I couldn't move. I was frozen in place. The spell book was about to fall out of my hands, but I couldn't clasp it tighter.

I couldn't swallow. I didn't know if I was breathing or not. I couldn't feel air enter or leave my nose. My chest certainly didn't move, couldn't move.

The book fell. My right thumb broke off and fell with it. I felt a moment of pure pain and then nothing. I had been turned to stone.

CHAPTER TWENTY

I COULD STILL HEAR the whippoorwill. I could still see, but I couldn't move my eyes or blink. I was staring at a shelf of books. *Hocus-pocus and Other Rhyming Incantations*; *Enemy Spells: Revenge Made Easy*; *Love Potions for Reluctant Lovers*; *Hex*; *The Complete Book of Wart Removal*; *Mistress Omonero's Remedies for Everything*.

Oh, how I wanted the next book on the shelf—*Spell Begone! A Thousand Release Spells*.

But who knew what a release spell would really do? It could turn me into a deer or a toad. A breathing, hopping toad might be an improvement.

I wondered if I was a beautiful statue or an ugly one. If I was beautiful and bore no resemblance to myself, no one would know what had become of me.

If I was still ugly, everyone would know.

I wanted to weep. It would be such a relief to weep! Or

to sing. I'd never sing again.

Mother and Father would never stop grieving.

I thought of the king. In a way, he was frozen, too.

I thought of Ijori. I couldn't stop thinking of him. My thoughts became as fixed on him as I was fixed in place. I thought of his ears, which Ivi disliked and I loved. I thought of his attachment to Oochoo and to his uncle. I thought of his high opinion of me. What a fool he'd think me now.

But if I had become beautiful—and not a statue—would he have loved me? Would he miss ugly me?

My candle guttered out. I was in pitch-darkness. Even the whippoorwill quieted. I had nothing except my thoughts.

I heard a chirp, then a coo, and the rustle of feathers. The library became murky rather than inky. Dawn was coming.

My scalp tingled. Then it itched. I couldn't move to scratch it. The tingle spread to my forehead, followed by the itch, then to my nose. I began to feel the air go in and out. I was able to raise my eyebrows. Oh, how glorious! To move my eyebrows. I'd never appreciated it before.

The spell was wearing off.

I felt fresh pain in my hand. Then my thumb flew up and reattached itself. I could move my arms. I scratched my ribs. I held out my hands. They were still broad, still meaty, still mottled. I was certain my face was still ugly, but never mind—I was glad to be flesh and not stone.

As I hurried through the sleeping castle, I felt something in my right slipper. In my chamber, I took off the slipper and my hose.

My right pinky toe was cold marble, through and through, white marble, the same chalky color as my skin. I tried to massage the toe back to life, but it wouldn't revert. I poured water on it, hoping it would become malleable again, but it didn't. I wrapped my fingers around it. It grew warmer but no softer. I stood and took several steps. It clicked on the wood floor beyond the rugs. It didn't chafe the toe next to it, but that toe was aware of it, the way you're aware if you tie a string around your finger.

I couldn't spend the day hunched over my toe. I straightened and dressed.

On my way to the Banquet Hall, I heard the jingle of Frying Pan's bracelets. Two guards were half dragging her along. She was in shackles. Her face was flushed. Her hair was loose. She roared out a song as she went.

> "Cook is a commoner,
> Born in her kitchen.
> The queen is from Kyrria,
> A commoner from Kyrria.

Cook goes to prison,
Queen goes to dinner.
Who will be the cook?
Isn't it an outrage?
Isn't it a crime?

"The king is lying sick.
The queen is sitting pretty.
The queen is making havoc
Upon the hungry court.
What's to eat tonight?
Eggshells, pig hair,
Scum, muck, and slime—
Isn't that a pity?
Isn't that a crime?"

I learned later that Lady Arona had also been imprisoned. Ivi had surmised that the plates of scraps had been
no mere prank and that Lady Arona had laughed at her.
Vengeance had been swift.

Imprisoning two subjects wasn't as bad as dissolving
the king's council or refusing to help with the drought, but
it felt as bad. It was so personal a use of power. She could
have demanded a public apology from each of them. The

humiliation would have been punishment enough.

The next morning Sir Enole, the physician, announced that the king's color had improved. The castle rang with song. Ivi asked me three times if I thought the king would like her gown. Twice she recited her favorite lines from his Wedding Song to her.

> "She makes me
> laugh and cry. . . .
> She wakes me up
> and makes me sing."

After the second recitation, she said, "Being a powerful queen is tiresome, Aza. Sometimes my head aches. I like much better to make Oscaro laugh and cry."

But everyone's joy over the king's rally turned to sadness when he failed to progress further. Even the songbirds sang in a minor key.

The castle fare deteriorated. Without Frying Pan, meals were late. The bread was stale. The cheese was moldy. Roasts were undercooked or burned. One memorable cake was frosted with chicken fat.

I received another letter from home, from Father this time. Word had reached Amonta that Ivi had dissolved the king's council and had refused to aid those suffering from the drought.

"*Daughter,*" he wrote,

> the mayor paid a visit to the Featherbed this morning, and I believe every soul in the village has come to your mother or to me. They entreat you to persuade Her Majesty to reverse her policies. When I brought my boots to Erdelle to be mended, he sent his apologies if he'd ever been unpleasant to you. Several guests have said the same.

I paused in my reading. I was surprised anyone felt guilt, and I couldn't help being pleased. They should have apologized long ago.

> In Amonta and here at the inn those who know you best are hopeful, because they're acquainted with your good heart. But among the others, anger against the queen runs high. Do your best, daughter. Your mother is becoming afraid.

I had no idea how to answer him. Good hearts weighed nothing with the queen.

CHAPTER TWENTY-ONE

*T*HE DAYS PASSED. Ivi kept her guards with her constantly. She seemed to fancy one guard more than the rest and flirted with him almost as much as she did with Ijori. His name was Uju, an older fellow than the others, so stern and silent that I couldn't tell how he was taking Ivi's attentions.

On occasion she visited the prison. She never took me, for which I was grateful. Once I heard her complain to the bailiff that Lady Arona and Frying Pan were being too well fed.

Frequently she shut herself in her apartments and ordered everyone to stay away. She didn't seem to have the temperament for solitude, but hours often passed before she summoned Ijori or me.

When she was busy and Ijori was not, he and I walked in the garden or watched the falconer train his birds or lazed on the bank of the moat. On one afternoon, he took me to the armory, a castle outbuilding not far from the lists. A manservant found us there and asked Ijori to go to Sir Uellu.

We walked back to the castle together. Ijori left me at the entrance, and I visited the tailor's booth to ask how my wardrobe was progressing. Mistress Audra, friendly as ever, assured me the sewing was going well.

The next day Ijori told me why he'd been called away. We stood on a stone terrace overlooking the Ormallo range. Oochoo sat between us. The slope across from us was dotted with sheep. The day was sweltering, with a hot dry breeze.

"Sir Uellu asked me what I think of you."

"What did you say?"

"I said I thought you honest, and kindly to a fault."

I wished I was honest.

"And he said about you—" Ijori looked pleased. "He said yours is the best voice he's ever heard, even better than Queen Adaria's."

She was the king's first wife, who'd died.

"He called yours an almost impossible voice. He said he thought you could do anything with it."

I tried not to sound alarmed. "He sent for you to talk about my voice?"

He grinned at me. "Why not? It deserves attention."

I blushed.

His grin faded. "The kingdom could soon be in revolt. The king's council continues to meet in secret. That is all I can tell you. Uellu asked where I would stand."

Revolt! My stomach knotted. I sat on the parapet. "But the king!"

He nodded. "Exactly. I said that as long as my uncle lives, I'll defend the queen."

"What did Sir Uellu say?"

"He said he would too."

"What will you do if your uncle should die?"

He stroked Oochoo's ear. "Oochoo would be a better queen than Queen Ivi. I'd oppose her." He bent over the dog. "What will you do, Aza? Queen Ivi is your patroness."

"I'd oppose her too." I'd finally be able to stop illusing. I'd be free of her. I wouldn't have to worry about the Featherbed, either. Mother and Father, too, would oppose the queen.

If the revolt failed, I'd be in prison with more company than Lady Arona and Frying Pan. Or I'd lose my head in the same good company.

He nodded. "I told Uellu you'd say just that."

Had Sir Uellu thought I'd support the queen?

"But," I said, "I hope King Oscaro gets well."

"Yes. Uncle . . ." He took a deep breath. "Sometimes I

wonder if he'd blame me for all that's happened."

"How could he blame you?"

"That I let her do what she would. That I let it come so close to rebellion."

I stood, indignant. "You tried to stop her! I tried. If you're at fault, so am I."

"Such spirit in my defense! Between you and Oochoo, I'm safe from any attack."

I laughed. "I will take up fencing."

He sobered. "Uncle's recovery would also save his wife."

I sobered too. A rebellion!

I woke up the next morning thinking about rebellion . . . and gowns. Today was to be my fitting. I was going to see my new ensembles and try them on. The alterations would be finished before the Sing. I would no longer be a laughingstock.

Today's Dame Ethele's monstrosity had a hooped under-skirt *and* a bustle that jutted out far behind me. In these skirts I could be a centaur and no one would ever know. Ah well, I thought, only one more day of shame.

I wished I could go straight to the tailor, but I had to help the queen dress. She was almost as excited as I was about the fitting. When she was ready, we set off for the tailor's stall together.

But trouble waylaid us when a blotch of whitish mush landed on her nose and dribbled onto to her chin and her lacy collar.

"What?" She began to reach up.

"Wait!" I said. "I'll get it." I dabbed at her face and collar with my handkerchief.

"It was a bird, wasn't it? Wasn't it?"

"I'm afraid so, Your Majesty."

She burst out, "I hate Ayortha!"

A courtier and a corridor troubadour were within earshot.

She took my handkerchief and rubbed at the stain. "Where else do they bring hordes of birds into a royal castle? My subjects are singing savages. Now I must decide on a different gown, although I so wanted to wear this one."

I turned back with her, but she put her hand on my arm. "You go ahead. I won't delay your moment."

She was always at her best when it came to apparel. If instead of a drought there had been a scarcity of fabric in the south, she would have been happy to open the king's coffers.

When I reached the tailor's stall, he turned away from his customer. The seamstresses looked up from their sewing. The courtiers stopped examining fabrics and patterns.

Mistress Audra's smile was overfriendly. "We are looking forward to seeing you in your new ensembles." She scurried behind the screen and emerged, staggering under the weight of a pile of garments.

The colors were garish.

She placed the garments on the fabrics table. The cloth was nothing I or the queen had selected. The uppermost gown was rich enough, but it was a stiff organdy in a violent shade of scarlet. Stitched into it were orange and green satin ruffles, rows of them. Stitched into the ruffles were bright-blue ribbons.

The other gowns were as bad. Textures and colors stabbed at me.

"We hope Milady likes her new wardrobe," the tailor said, smirking.

"The queen won't pay for these." I wouldn't let them see me cry.

The tailor bowed. "Consider them a gift. They will adorn you as you deserve."

I left everything. As soon as I turned away, my eyes filled. I wanted to be alone in my chamber. People stood aside as I rushed toward the staircase at the back of the hall.

I heard someone behind me.

"Aza!"

Ijori. I didn't want to see him now. I ran. I reached the staircase and started up.

He came after me. "Aza! What's amiss?"

I climbed as rapidly as I could, but Dame Ethele's skirts slowed me. He put his hand on my elbow. At least I was high enough to be out of sight of the Great Hall. I sank on a step and began to sob.

"What? What happened?"

But I was crying too hard to speak.

He sat on the step below me. He reached up to pat my shoulder and my back. He murmured, "Don't cry. What is it? Nothing's so bad. Don't cry, sweet. Oh, dear heart, don't cry."

Sweet? Dear heart? I turned to him. What was he saying?

He rose and came closer and kissed my blood-red mouth.

CHAPTER TWENTY-TWO

*H*IS LIPS FELT SO soft.

I'd thought I'd grow old and die without ever a kiss. A melody bloomed in my mind, high and clear and joyous. He was kissing me.

He drew away, a little away, and smoothed the hair from my face. He murmured, "You smell like a meadow."

I touched his cheek. I hummed the melody my mind was singing. He smiled and listened.

After a while I stopped humming, but the tune continued in my mind.

"Why were you crying?"

"It doesn't matter anymore." It didn't.

"It does matter. Someone was cruel."

I shrugged.

"They don't know you." He sang, "I know you. You're

the finest, kindest, sweetest maiden in Ayortha." He kissed me again.

A prince could judge ostumo.

Then Oochoo was there, sticking her snout between us, wagging her tail, licking Ijori's face and mine. We both stood, laughing. He returned to the hall and I proceeded up the stairs. My mind went back to singing.

The queen would expect me to be a while at the fitting. I could go to my room and calm myself.

I stopped climbing. Ivi would recognize that the tailor's behavior had been an insult to her. Without a doubt she'd imprison him, and probably Mistress Audra as well. They had been even more rash than Frying Pan. They'd known what the queen might do.

But I didn't want them imprisoned. I wanted my new wardrobe. They deserved punishment, but not imprisonment. I had to save them if I could. I started back down the stairs, considering how I might manage the tailor.

He bowed when I reached his stall. "Milady has returned for her finery."

I snapped out, "Come with me." I had never played the great lady before, but I'd watched the duchess.

He followed me behind a pillar, where we could have relative privacy.

I drew myself up to my full height, half a foot above his

head. Ijori's kiss had fortified me. "You thought to have fun with the queen's favorite and be safe from the queen herself."

"Milady—"

"Her Majesty intended to come with me. If she had, you and your seamstresses would be in prison now. Did you think of Mistress Audra and the others?"

"It was—"

"And, with you in prison, tomorrow the tailor from Ontio town will set up his stall in your place."

His face reddened. "The tailor Emoree? That charl—"

I nodded. "Yes, that charlatan. Or perhaps Her Majesty will send for a Kyrrian tailor from her hometown of Bast."

The tailor looked apoplectic.

"Did you think about that?" I sang. "Did you think at all? But"—I returned to speech—"if my wardrobe is finished, you will keep your stall and no one will be thrown in the dungeon."

"We will make it up for you." He didn't meet my eyes.

"Look at me!"

He looked up.

"I want it in time for the Sing, and I want the ensembles I chose, in the fabrics I chose."

"You will have them, but—"

I barked out, "But what?"

"—there will be no time for a fitting."

"Then see that everything is perfect."

"Yes, milady. Milady?"

"Yes?"

"What will you tell the queen?"

"I'll tell Her Majesty that you are putting on the finishing touches."

"Tell her, too, that she won't find a tailor of my quality anywhere in Ontio or Kyrria."

"If I like my new ensembles, I'll certainly tell her that. Indeed, she'll see for herself. Good day, Tailor." I strode away, feeling a thousand feet tall, and glad to be, for the first time in my life.

Kisses were better than potions.

When I reached Ivi's chambers, I told her the fitting had gone well, and everything would be ready in time for the Sing.

She clapped her hands. "Which will you wear? I know! Wear the blue brocade. No, don't wear it. Bring it here. Bring all your new finery. You'll wait on me and I'll wait on you. I'll be your lady-in-waiting, and you'll be mine. We'll look so splendid, the court will go blind from the sight of us. It almost makes me like Sings."

In the Throne Room that afternoon she flirted with the two guards, but especially with the guard Uju. Ijori and I wrote our songs while Oochoo dozed. I wrote Ivi's song as well as my own. I'd asked her if I might, and, to my surprise, she'd said yes.

It was hard to pay attention to writing with Ijori only a few feet away. I sat near the fireplace and leaned on a slate I'd found on the hearth. He sat at the desk where, he said, the king penned his proclamations.

I wanted to move my chair closer to his. I wanted to do nothing but smile at him. Neither would be wise. Ivi wouldn't want me making sheep's eyes at her prince.

And she wouldn't want him making sheep's eyes at me, which I saw he was in danger of doing. I lowered my head and concentrated on my song.

I wrote about my feeling for beauty, for being beautiful.

This was my song.

> *There are those*
> *who find solace*
> *in a twisted oak,*
> *who can love*
> *the maggot in a pear.*
> *But I adore*
> *the plum that has no worm,*
> *the song that comes out pure,*
> *the shine of a polished stone,*

the chick with the deepest down.
There are those who love the rain.
Not I.
I love the cloudless sky.

There are those
who long to ease
a sick dame's steps,
who ache to trim
an old man's beard.
But I yearn
for a golden feather,
for the greenest leaf,
the scent of a sleeping child,
the circle of a perfect peach.
Some love the rain.
Not I.
I love the cloudless sky.

When you think of me,
remember how I yearned,
remember how I ached.
Know how I longed
to be
a bright blue sky.

But I no longer wanted the bright blue sky so much. I had something better.

Now for the queen's song. A sung apology would be received best. But she'd never sing—or mouth the words of—such a song.

Second best would be a song about missing the king. I knew the way she missed him. She missed his love for her. She missed being the reason for his laughter and his tears.

But her subjects wouldn't like that. The song should be about the way they would want her to miss him. I wrote:

> *Ayortha, I miss my lord.*
> *I miss my heart that still*
> *Lives in his chest.*
> *I miss—*

"Do not write too long a song." Ivi stood at my shoulder.

"I won't, Your Majesty." I wished she'd move away. I couldn't write with her watching.

"Many Ayorthaian songs are far too long, don't you agree, Prince Ijori?"

He smiled noncommittally. "The composer and the hearer often have different opinions on that score."

She returned to Uju. "Uju agrees with me. They are too long, no?"

He shrugged.

She quizzed Uju about his song and received the shortest of replies. In a few minutes she gave up and announced she was retiring to her chambers. She left, accompanied by the two guards.

Ijori put his writing aside and came to me. He sang, "Sing to me."

I sang, "What shall I sing?"

"Anything."

I sang, "Four thousand seven hundred and thirty-eight. Four thousand seven hundred and thirty-nine. Four thousand seven hundred and forty."

He laughed. "It sounds marvelous when you sing it. I'll sing, too. Four thousand seven hundred . . ."

I joined in. "And forty-one. Four thousand seven hundred and forty-two. Four—"

A servant came in. Sir Uellu wanted the prince again.

Ijori conquered his laughter, touched my shoulder, and left. He could hardly do more with the servant there, but I wished for another kiss.

A noise woke me in the middle of the night before the Sing. I heard muffled banging. I thought of getting up to investigate, but I drifted back to sleep instead.

In the morning something was different. I threw off the bedclothes. I put on my shift and sang:

"Climb the day,
Drop your dreams."

I stopped. I knew what the difference was. The birds weren't singing.

CHAPTER TWENTY-THREE

I THREW ON DAME Ethele's shawl and poked my head out my door.

There were no birds. I usually saw one or two flying and several others perched on the sconces or the door frames.

The bird droppings! She'd taken revenge.

I dressed hurriedly. The Great Hall was full of people standing still, staring up. As I threaded through the crowd, I heard a sob, a few lines of song. A man spat at me as I hurried by. I wasn't thinking about my wardrobe, but the tailor called my name.

I turned.

He thrust an enormous bundle at me, wrapped in canvas. "It is done." His false smile was gone. "I know you are not to blame."

I said, "Were the birds killed?"

"Not killed. Released outside." He raised an eyebrow. "They'll be back."

I felt better.

"When they come back," he said, "we'll make sure they stay."

I felt worse. The rebellion.

He added, "We did our best with the wardrobe. The gowns will help you look less . . ." He trailed off.

Less hideous.

Ivi opened her eyes sleepily when I came in. But she sat up when she saw the bundle in my arms.

"Your wardrobe!" She slid over. "Let me see."

I set the bundle down next to her. "Your Majesty, the birds—"

"I couldn't abide them. Filthy things."

"Your subjects . . . the king—"

"Oh, don't reproach me, Aza. Even if the king was well, dirt would be my domain. Fetch my scissors."

She cut the string and pulled apart the canvas covering.

"Oh," I breathed.

She lifted up the top gown, a pale yellow crepe with a tiny ruffle at the waist and cuffs. "Show me."

I took it from her and went behind her screen. I had just unbuttoned the top button of my bodice when she said querulously, "My breakfast?"

I buttoned the bodice again. "I forgot!"

"Fetch it now. How could you have been so heedless?"

She could have let me put on one of the new gowns. I laid the crepe carefully over a chair back.

The hallways were bleak without birdsong. The corridor troubadours were silent too. My footfalls were somber drumbeats.

When I returned with her breakfast, my ensembles were spread out on her bed. A gold chain lay across the bodice of one. Silver beads and pearls lay across another. There were also an opal pendant hung on a velvet ribbon, a garnet brooch, a lace collar, and three gold rings.

"Oh!" I stood at the head of the bed, blinking at the jewelry.

Ivi was at the foot of the bed, looking happier than I'd seen her since her wedding. "They're yours. I want you to have them."

She took the breakfast tray from me and set it down on the desk. "Aza," she said solemnly, "thank you for being the best lady-in-waiting a queen could ever hope for."

"Thank you." Was she about to demand something dreadful of me?

She put both hands on my shoulders. "Aza?"

"Yes, Your Majesty."

"Do you care about me?"

I cared what she did to me. "Of course, Your Majesty."

"Deeply? Do you care about me deeply?"

She was going to make me do something to prove I cared. I nodded and waited.

But she let me go and picked up my violet silk gown. Holding it against herself, she said, "I have too many jewels, and don't you think I matched them perfectly with the ensembles? You must admit my taste is nonpareil."

"Your taste is marvelous." Did she want only admiration?

"Don a gown! Try a necklace! Show me!"

Again I went behind her screen. I removed the hooped farthingale and left the thin underskirt. I picked up the crepe gown, suddenly certain the fabric was too delicate for me. I should never have chosen anything so destructible. I raised my arms and drew the skirt over my head. It fluttered down to my hips as gently as rose petals.

While I dressed, Ivi prattled happily. She'd thought of a new way to arrange my hair. She wasn't sure which gown she should wear tonight, and which was my favorite color? Hers was gold. Which did I think Prince Ijori preferred?

She recited the favorite colors of several youths in her hometown of Bast. "They were all my beaus. I had more beaus than anyone. No minxes ever took them from me. Hurry and show me how you look."

The gown fit perfectly. I stepped out from behind the screen.

"Oh, Aza. It's magnificent." She jumped up from the bed. "You can't look until I do something with your hair. Close your eyes."

She sat me in the dressing table chair and fussed over me. I wished I could look into Skulni and perhaps see my beautified self in my new gown.

"Mmm . . . you're ready for the cap."

The headdress for the ensemble was a simple circle of lined cloth with a tiny brim. She set it in place. "Now, rise and admire yourself. No. Wait." She turned me away from the mirror.

I opened my eyes. She flew to the bed for the garnet brooch. She held it here, held it there, and finally placed it below the wispy collar.

In spite of the new gown I was reluctant to look in the mirror, but I did—not in Skulni, but in the ordinary mirror above the dressing table.

I was still too white and too red and too black. But I appeared less bulky. The crinkles of the crepe ran on the bias. The result was a spiral that made my waist slimmer and my hips narrower. The tailor was a master.

Ivi had tucked most of my hair under the cap and had left only a single coil showing. The effect was to make my face less round and to suggest that somewhere, under a pound of fleshy cheeks, I had cheekbones. Ivi was also a master.

She decided that we should devote the rest of the day to fashion. She had me try on every gown, and she modeled each of her gowns for me.

I missed Ijori.

In the afternoon I grew nervous about illusing at the Sing. I actually persuaded Ivi to pause and rehearse her song with me.

She remembered the words. Everything should go well. I had illused for her many times. But I was still uneasy.

Ijori and Oochoo were waiting for us at the entrance to the Hall of Song. Ivi wore a turquoise gown, and mine was midnight blue. She'd caught my hair up in a shimmering blue net and had hung the gold chain around my neck.

Ijori bowed and said, "Blue becomes you . . . both."

But he was looking at me.

I blushed and lost any advantage the gown gave me.

Ivi said, "A good tailor can perform wonders."

He smiled. "If he has someone extraordinary to perform them upon."

My blush was blushing.

Ivi frowned. "That's my hairnet Aza is wearing."

He bowed again.

We entered the Hall of Song. I missed the birds. Sir Uellu announced there would be a toast after the queen sang her song. No sign of pleasure greeted the announcement. The mood in the hall was leaden.

My mood was livelier. Fright is livelier than lead.

The first song was always the Song of Ayortha, sung by everyone.

Sir Uellu held up his hand. "Tonight we will depart from custom for a rare treat. Her Majesty and Lady Aza will sing the Song of Ayortha as a duet."

I took a half step to run from the hall.

"Choirmaster!" Ivi wet her lips. "I forgot my promise! Alas, I cannot perform unrehearsed. I simply cannot. We'll begin the next Sing with the duet."

Sir Uellu nodded as if he'd expected her answer. He raised his baton, and we all began the Three Tree Song. The singing lagged a quarter beat behind his baton. Sir Uellu slowed to let us catch up, and we slowed too, until the song was a dirge.

Next he led us in a lively river song, but that felt dull and lifeless, too. He signaled for our solos, although the choral portion of a Sing generally lasts two hours. Ijori frowned, but no one else seemed to care.

A footman sang about his favorite cap, a groom about his collection of horse collars. Several people yawned.

Others coughed or shifted restlessly. I chewed on my cheek to keep from exploding. A knight sang. It would be my turn soon. Two ladies sang. It was my turn. I mounted the stage.

I wanted to sing directly to Ijori, but I didn't look at him. Out of the corner of my eye, however, I saw him sway as soon as I began. The guards shook their heads happily. Ivi swayed awkwardly, but everyone else was rigid. I was singing well. They were resisting . . .

. . . except Sir Uellu, who was swaying and shaking his head and smiling.

> "When you think of me,
>   remember how I yearned,
>   remember how I ached.
>   Know how I longed
>   to be
>   a bright blue sky."

I finished. When I reached my seat, Ijori whispered, "The best of the night."

Surreptitiously, I found his hand and held it in the folds of my skirts.

The songs continued. Many were too short. They were an insult to the queen, although I'm sure she was grateful for the brevity. She was staring at nothing and smiling fixedly.

Ijori was next. He let my hand go and climbed up to the stage.

> *"This should be the saddest time*
> *when someone I love—*
> *my uncle—*
> *when something happens . . .*
> *my heart should die. . . .*
>
> *"This should be the gladdest time*
> *with someone to love—*
> *my dear friend—*
> *when that happens . . .*
> *my heart should fly. . . ."*

He was singing to everyone, but the song was a gift for me. I swayed and shook my head and beamed. His eyes met mine briefly. Then he continued to sing to everyone.

Ivi was rocking back and forth rather than swaying. She was furious. She knew the song wasn't for her, although I doubt she knew it was for me.

> *"I smile and cry*
> *and wish the love had come*

> *without the sorrow,*
> *because they're now combined,*
> *entwined in my marrow,*
> *sprouting from my fingers,*
> *pouring from my lips,*
> *sorrow and joy*
> *love and love*
> *love and love."*

He left the stage and returned to his seat. We joined hands again.

Ijori's mother, Princess Elainee, sang. My nervousness mounted. Ivi came next.

Sir Uellu nodded, and several servants left the hall. I assumed they had something to do with the toast, and sure enough, while Princess Elainee finished her song, they filed back in, carrying goblets of mead.

Ivi mounted the stage. The serving maids moved through the hall, distributing drinks.

Ivi licked her lips. I thought of not singing and letting her send me to prison. She opened her mouth, and I came in.

> *"Ayortha, I miss my lord.*
> *I miss my heart that still*
> *lives . . ."*

A serving maid climbed to the stage to bring Ivi her drink.

> " . . . in his chest.
> I miss his whisper in my ear . . ."

Behind me there was a crash and the sound of breaking glass. Oochoo jumped up. Still illusing, I turned around, along with everyone else, to see what had happened. I sang,

> "Saying, This is Ayortha.
> This is our home . . ."

just as Ivi yelled, "You clumsy fool. You—"

Everyone turned back to gape at the queen, who had mead running down the front of her gown as she shrieked and sang at the same time.

CHAPTER TWENTY-FOUR

*I*T WOULD ALL come out now. I turned to Ijori. "I had to. I didn't want to."

Ivi was still yelling at the serving maid. "You ninny, see what you've done?"

She would blame me and send me to prison. Mother and Father would lose the Featherbed. I felt the tears come.

Ivi cried, "Oh!" in a surprised voice. Then, "Oh, I forgot to sing. I'll resume." She looked at me, and then she must have noticed the quality of the silence.

After a moment's pause she shrilled, "I'm sick of singing Ayorthaians. Every day I have a headache. Oscaro wouldn't want me to have headaches." She gathered herself and then announced, "From now on there will be no more Sings in Ayortha and no more singing in the castle."

She ran off the stage and out of the hall. Uju began to

follow her, then thought better of it. The other guards didn't move.

I let go of Ijori's hand and rushed after her. I had to apologize for continuing to sing. I had to beg her to take pity on Mother and Father.

She heard me behind her. She whirled and screamed, "Bungler, monster!"

"Your Majesty, please—"

"Go away, fright!" She started running again. "Leave me alone, horror!"

I stopped and turned around. Ijori was in the doorway of the Hall of Song. I went to him, and we stepped back inside.

Everyone had crowded into the space between the stage and the seats. They were talking or shouting or singing. Several people sang that they'd never stop singing. Others wondered what magic Ivi had performed to both sing and speak at once.

Sir Uellu's voice sliced through the hubbub. He sang, "Will the other members of the king's council come with me? Lady Aza, please come." He turned. "Bailiff?"

The bailiff, a gray-haired, stocky man, swam through the crowd.

"Master Ebbe," Sir Uellu said, "please come, too."

I wondered if the bailiff was for Ivi. Or for me. Or for both of us.

Princess Elainee and Master Ogusso, a music illuminator, joined us. Master Ogusso was the commoner on the council. The choirmaster and the prince were also members, and the queen made the council complete.

A scullery maid began the first line of the Song of Ayortha. Everyone joined in, singing with the spirit that had been lacking all night. They were singing as we left. Oochoo stopped licking up spilled mead and loped after us.

The bailiff's pike clanged against the tile floor with each step he took. I felt the clanging in my bones.

Ijori walked next to me. I wanted to explain before Ivi started lying. "I didn't want to sing for her. I tried to refuse."

"Swee— Lady Aza, what do you mean, you sang for her?"

Sir Uellu said, "All will be explained very soon. Lady Aza, please wait."

I was afraid to wait, but I said no more.

Princess Elainee looked around the echoing corridor. "How could she have taken our birds? They never hurt her."

No one answered.

Ijori touched my arm. He asked Sir Uellu, "Why do you need Lady Aza?"

The choirmaster only said, "Soon."

He knew everything. My steps flagged.

He said, "Come, Lady Aza."

We reached the royal wing of the castle. As we approached Ivi's door, it flew open. Oochoo ran ahead. The rest of us stopped.

"Finally!" Ivi appeared in the doorway and saw us. She edged away from Oochoo and drew herself up. "Oh. I didn't call for you, but the bailiff and Prince Ijori may stay."

Sir Uellu continued toward her, singing, "Your Majesty issued a command tonight that will never be obeyed."

Her voice rose. "Don't sing at me! Bailiff, I want my guards."

Master Ebbe said, "Your Majesty—"

Sir Uellu cut him off. "There is much to be spoken of before we speak of guards." He swept past her, into her chambers.

We followed. Ivi stood defiantly in the center of the room. Ijori remained with me just inside the door. The only light came from two candles in sconces over the dressing table. I noticed that Skulni was on the dressing table. Sir Uellu began to light a lamp on the mantelpiece.

"How dare you! I don't want a light."

He ignored her and won the upper hand. The defiance went out of her stance, and she became disarmingly fragile.

I wished I could do that. She looked piteous, and I was going to need pity.

With the change in Ivi, much of the tension left the

chamber. Princess Elainee and Master Ogusso seated themselves, she in the easy chair, he on the ottoman.

I sat on a stool at the foot of the bed. Ijori stood over me protectively. Oochoo rested her head in my lap.

Sir Uellu rocked back on his heels and folded his arms. "Your Majesty, Lady Aza has been singing for you, am I correct?"

Ijori took a step away from me.

So quickly. So readily.

"Yes." Ivi's voice was small and childlike. She sat on the bench by the fireplace and looked up at him. "You've found her out. Yes."

Found *me* out?

Master Ogusso said, "Singing for someone? What chicanery is that?"

"I suspect," Sir Uellu said, "that our queen's voice is worse than mediocre."

"No one here would like it," Ivi said in the same small voice. "But in other kingdoms they might."

Princess Elainee said, "How do you sing for someone, Lady Aza?"

I put my hand in front of my face. "It's . . . I . . ." My throat closed.

Sir Uellu went to Ivi's washstand and poured a tumbler of water from the pitcher. "Here."

I drank. "I call it illusing."

Ijori sang, "Did Her Majesty command you to do it?"

I nodded. "She threatened to close the Featherbed and throw me in prison."

"She's lying!" Ivi said. "She said she'd sing for me if I'd make her my lady-in-waiting. That's what she really said."

It sounded so true, obvious even.

Sir Uellu turned to the bailiff. "Master Ebbe, we have need of several guards."

For me?

Master Ebbe bowed to Sir Uellu and left.

"How do you do your illusing?" Ijori said. His voice softened. "Aza . . ." He changed his mind. "Don't lie."

"I never wanted to lie." I swallowed back tears and described illusing.

Master Ogusso asked Sir Uellu, "Is this possible?"

"Show us," Sir Uellu said.

"Wait." The tears came. I couldn't illuse and weep at the same time. I sipped more water.

Ivi said, "She showed me right after Oscaro . . . after my lord . . ."

I placed the tumbler on the floor. Princess Elainee jumped as I illused in her speaking voice, "Aza hated tricking people."

Oochoo raised her head and barked.

The princess said, "I didn't say that!"

Ijori said, "Then why didn't you tell me?"

I deepened my voice to imitate Master Ogusso. "Aza was frightened."

Master Ogusso sang, "This is astonishing."

"How do you do it?" Princess Elainee asked.

I shook my head, too distressed to answer.

They waited.

Finally I said, "I'm not sure." I paused. "It started with the hiccups."

While I was explaining, Master Ebbe returned with three guards. One stood at the door to the chamber, one at the door to the wardrobe closet and the king's empty bedchamber, and one loomed over me.

The council members tried to illuse—all except Ijori, who went to the window and stared out into the night.

I wished I could illuse words into his mouth and make him mean them, words like "I believe you." Words like "I know you too well to think you'd enjoy duping people." Words like "dear heart, sweet, love."

He said, "Oochoo, come."

She went to him, wagging her tail. He patted her head. She licked his hand and then returned to me and curled up at my feet.

A dog could judge ostumo.

"I can't illuse," Master Ogusso said, giving up. "My throat must be arranged differently from hers."

Princess Elainee said, "Even if Lady Aza sang for Her Majesty tonight, Queen Ivi herself commanded us not to sing."

"She told me to!" Ivi said, glaring at me. "She said that if we were ever found out, I should distract everyone by ordering them not to sing."

"We never spoke of being found out."

Ijori's back was to the room, but I saw him watch my reflection in the window.

I sang:

> *"I'm an*
> *innkeeper's daughter.*
> *An honest inn,*
> *the Featherbed.*
> *No rooms for*
> *deceivers."*

"I don't believe Her Majesty was blameless," Sir Uellu said. "She was weak, certainly, and—"

"I was powerful!"

". . . and her judgment was poor. However, a pernicious influence was at work, which even a stronger mind couldn't resist." His gaze shifted to Ijori.

"What influence?" Princess Elainee asked. "Whose influence?"

I wondered if Sir Uellu had identified the advisor Ivi sometimes spoke of.

"I can now explain both the illusing and the extraordinary rise to prominence of an innkeeper's daughter."

My heart rose into my throat.

"Lady Aza's voice has power and range beyond anything I've heard." He looked in turn at Master Ogusso, Princess Elainee, and Ijori. "What quality do several of the best singers in Ayorthaian history share?"

Ijori looked blank, then shook his head vehemently.

Princess Elainee said, "Oh!" in a shocked voice.

Master Ogusso said, "You mean . . . ?"

Sir Uellu nodded. "They had a drop or two of ogre blood in their veins."

I felt as if I was falling. I remembered the library keeper singing about Queen Amba: that she had a marvelous voice, and people thought she was an ogre's great-granddaughter.

Sir Uellu was still speaking. "Lady Aza, I suspect, has more than a few drops of ogre blood. She may be an ogre's first cousin. I had only to hear her and look at her to think it."

CHAPTER TWENTY-FIVE

*I*VI LOOKED SURPRISED and delighted.

I had never felt such fury. I stood and sang, flooding the room with sound. "I am no ogre!"

But I wasn't sure.

I lowered my voice and spoke. "I am no traitor."

Ijori stared at me, as they all did, as if I were a creature in a menagerie.

I sang, flooding the room again, "I am loyal to Ayortha-a-a-a-a." I held the *a*, made it reverberate against the walls.

Oochoo barked. The bailiff nodded at the guards. I continued to blare forth. A guard advanced on me. I stopped singing.

Ijori sang, his voice full of horror. "I kissed you!"

I hated him.

Both Ivi and Princess Elainee cried, "You kissed her?"

"I wish you hadn't," I said. "Someone as faithless as you."

At least he looked disconcerted.

"She can't be allowed to do this illusing," Princess Elainee said. "We can't trust our ears."

"She did worse than illusing," Sir Uellu said. He addressed me. "You won the queen's affections and gave her advice that would cause a rebellion."

"Rebellion!" Ivi cried.

I sank onto the bed. "I didn't! I wouldn't! Why would I?"

"Ah!" Sir Uellu said. "Because you'd also insinuated yourself into the prince's affections. The queen would be overthrown. You'd marry the prince and become queen."

The room was spinning.

"He'd marry *her*?" Ivi said.

Ijori said softly, "I'd hoped to wed her."

"Oh, son," Princess Elainee said.

I was going to faint, or retch. I lowered my head to my lap.

"Wed her?" Ivi said. "Wed her! Guards! Imprison her."

My stomach churned. I stood and lurched to the wash-stand. Oochoo came with me. As I threw up into the basin, the others decided it would be too dangerous to consider my fate in my presence. The bailiff stationed guards outside. The council and Ivi exited into the king's bedchamber. Ijori called Oochoo, and she left me.

I was alone. I collapsed onto the rug. I closed my eyes and

didn't move for a long while.

If I'd been pretty, I'd have been safe. If I'd had an ordinary voice, I'd have been safe. I dragged myself up and went to Ivi's dressing table. Ugly, in the ordinary mirror. Ogreish? Maybe.

I looked into Skulni, and my face became beautiful. No trace of ogre in that face. How I'd love to be beautiful when Ijori and the rest returned! I'd laugh at their shock. I'd laugh and laugh.

The image faded. I pulled open the dressing table drawer. I'd looked in it a thousand times, and I found no potion now either. I stared down at the tabletop, at the cosmetics and the mirror and the golden flute. Why would a woman who had no music in her keep a flute on her dressing table?

I knew why.

I unscrewed the flute's mouthpiece. Two small vials slid into my shaking hand. One was made of green clay, the other brown. Neither was much bigger than my thumb. Each bore a label. The green vial's label read "Beauty." The other label read "Disguises."

I uncorked the green vial and raised it to my lips.

How much should I drink? I lowered the vial, aware of my marble toe.

I wondered when the others would return.

The tumbler Sir Uellu had brought me was on the floor by the bed, still half filled with water. I carried the vial to it and tipped in four drops. The potion was clear, but the water turned cloudy. I returned to the dressing table and emptied the draft down my throat. It was mildly salty, nothing worse.

I watched myself in the ordinary mirror, not in the hand mirror. I wanted an honest reflection.

Nothing changed. Perhaps it had no magic for humans with ogre blood.

A blaze ripped through me, from my scalp to my toes. My eyes watered and burned. I ran to the washstand and threw the water left in the pitcher on myself. The fire roared on. I saw my hand holding the pitcher. The skin was red and coarse, the texture and color of a tongue.

The fire passed. But then my bones, my muscles, my bowels, my heart, were squeezed and twisted, wrung, as if by a giant washerwoman. I felt myself fall. Then I felt nothing.

I awoke on the floor, free of pain. I saw a section of rug, my sleeve, my wrist, and my hand. I moved a finger to prove it was my hand. It didn't look like my hand. It was too pretty.

The finger moved.

I flew to the mirror. There I was—my beautified face—in the ordinary mirror. And not merely my face—my neck was graceful, and my shoulders were narrower. I was commanding, but no longer oppressive.

The midnight-blue gown had become too big, and it was wet around the shoulders where I'd tried to douse myself. I was glorious in the gown nonetheless. I would be glorious in a potato sack.

I smiled at my image. Oh, such a smile! A wounded bird's spirits would lift at that smile.

I sang softly,

> *"Some love the rain*
> *Not I.*
> *I love the cloudless sky."*

I had become the cloudless sky. I wondered if my marble toe had become flesh again. I concentrated. No, it was still marble.

Perhaps I could win Ijori back. He couldn't hate me when I looked like this. He'd listen to me now.

But I hated him.

"You are fairest now, fairer than . . ."

I spun around, but no one was there. I spun back and

looked down and saw a face in the hand mirror. The creature in the mirror. Skulni!

He had a man's face, a sharp face—small features and small ears and a nose that came to a point. He was smiling at me, his eyes slits of merry spite.

"Fairer than Queen Ivi. You are the fairest one of all."

His voice was flat, with no music. It was sugary and insinuating, the voice of a spider inviting a fly in for ostumo.

"Finish the potion, Lady Aza, or your beauty will be fleeting."

I touched my ivory cheek. I didn't want to revert.

But I didn't trust him, and I didn't want to burn up again or be squeezed again.

"Hurry! They'll be back soon."

I opened my reticule and dropped in the vial. I'd decide later.

"When you leave this room, the vial will remain. The potions stay with the mirror. Drink up."

I took the vial back out of the reticule.

"Drink." He chuckled. "Or your love will return and see you change from fair to frightful."

He was too eager. I put both vials back in the flute. "Four drops will suffice."

What were they deciding about me in the king's chambers? What was Ijori saying?

Skulni said, "If you finish the vial, I can tell you my plans for Ayortha and the queen."

I didn't know what he was talking about, and I didn't care.

I did care.

"Tell me. Then I'll finish it."

I heard voices and bustle in the wardrobe closet. I turned to face the door. I wanted to see their expressions when they saw me.

Oochoo ran to me. She didn't seem to notice any change. She greeted me, and I petted her. Had I reverted in the last second?

Ijori came in first, but he hadn't yet taken me in when Ivi shrieked. She ran past him and—before I could protect myself—slapped me across the face.

CHAPTER TWENTY-SIX

Oochoo growled and barked at Ivi. I reeled back and put my hand to my stinging cheek. Ivi edged away from Oochoo.

Ijori said, "Aza . . ." He looked away from me and then looked back, as if he doubted his eyes. "Aza, what . . ."

Princess Elainee said, "Am I dreaming?"

"Did someone take her place?" Master Ogusso said. "She's so beautiful." He added, "But I think she's still Lady Aza—Maid Aza now."

I was no longer a lady. No matter.

Ivi came at me again. Oochoo lunged at her.

"Don't let your dog bite me!" She ran to Ijori.

I sang, "Do you still see my ogre blood, Sir Uellu?"

He said, "What caused your transformation?"

I didn't answer. I owed them no explanations.

Sir Uellu opened the door to the corridor. The bailiff and

the two guards came in.

"She's so beautiful," Master Ogusso repeated. "I can't tear my eyes away from her."

"She's too tall," Ivi said. "Like a giraffe."

"She's perfect," Master Ogusso said.

The bailiff nodded at the guards. They came toward me, boots thudding, swords rattling, both men bigger than even I used to be. One had a grim mouth.

Oochoo growled and barked.

Ijori took her by the collar and pulled her away from me. "It's all right, girl."

He was letting them take me.

I tried to run, but the guards grabbed me and held me. The one with the grim mouth kept tightening his grip.

"Gently!" Ijori said.

"What are you doing with me?"

Ivi came to me, brave now that Ijori was holding Oochoo and the guards were holding me. "Aza. Aza. Aza. I thought we were such friends. My heart breaks, the way you've treated me. I have a tender heart, and now it's broken."

Sir Uellu said, "For the safety of Ayortha, the guards will take you to prison."

Prison after all! I sang, "For how long?"

"We haven't determined yet," Princess Elainee said. "But we cannot leave you free to illuse and confuse us."

"What of my parents' inn, the Featherbed?"

Sir Uellu said, "Your family has done nothing wrong."

Ijori said, "The crown will be generous."

"Why should it be?" Ivi asked.

"It will be," Ijori said firmly.

The guards gagged me and bound my hands.

"You may take her away now," Sir Uellu said.

The gag tore at the corners of my mouth. I started a tune in my mind as they walked me out of Ivi's chambers, a brave tune, with trumpets and many voices. It stayed with me through the castle corridors. I thought of Frying Pan being taken to prison.

> *Isn't it an outrage?*
> *Isn't it a crime?*

My courage lasted until we descended into the cellar. The air that belched up from below was rank. The stone stairs were slippery. I might have fallen if not for the guards' grip on my elbows. How was I to live down there?

The stairs ended. All I could see of the tunnel ahead was a small circle illumined by the guards' lanterns. The tunnel was hewn from solid rock, with thick timber supports every few paces. The walls glistened with slime. A rat scurried out of the light.

After several hundred yards the tunnel turned right. My steps flagged. My legs felt as if they, too, were rock. The guards towed me along. Eventually we reached a wooden door reinforced with iron.

The bailiff unlocked the door.

Four tallow lamps burned in sconces near the low ceiling. Beneath one of them a ring of keys hung on a nail. Six iron cell doors were set in three walls. There was a window in each door, striped by iron bars.

Mounted on a wall between cell doors were iron manacles and a cat-o'-nine-tails. A lunatic's cage, big enough for a lion, stood in the middle of the floor.

A screen in one corner gave the guard privacy to use the chamber pot. A brazier of glowing coals on a wrought-iron stand dispelled some of the damp chill.

The prison guard rose from his wooden table. "Never had such a pretty prisoner before."

I'd longed for admiration. Now I had it.

Frying Pan appeared in one of the cell windows. "Is that the innkeeper's daughter? Did Her Maj— What happened to the wench?"

Lady Arona appeared in another window and stared out at me.

"I want this one where you can see her every second, Izzi," the bailiff told the prison guard. "Put her in the cage."

Cage! There was a drumming in my ears. I stamped on my right-hand guard's foot and yanked my arm free. I punched my other guard in the eye and jerked out of his grip. He staggered back. I had lost none of my former strength.

My mind sharpened. I noticed that Izzi, the prison guard, favored his left leg and that the hot brazier could be a weapon.

I lunged for the prison door. A guard slammed it shut. He reached for me. I made a battering ram of my head and charged at the bailiff. Head met stomach, and he went down. I bounded toward the brazier.

A guard vaulted to the top of the cage and then leaped onto my shoulders. I fell. The others descended on me.

The bailiff rose and dusted himself off. "Take care with her, Izzi. She's part ogre."

Izzi opened the cage, and the other guards shoved me inside. They slammed the door and shot home the bolt an instant before I threw myself against the bars. My mind was roaring. But the observant part of me noticed the bolt. No key, just a bolt. And then I caught a weakness in the cage. I threw myself at the bars again. They held against me.

I squatted—there was no room to stand—and lowered my head to my lap.

I heard the bailiff release Frying Pan and Lady Arona.

Their freedom would infuriate Ivi, but she would have to heed the council now. I heard everyone leave, all but Izzi. The door thudded shut.

"I'd let you out if I dared, sweet. I'd unbind your mouth and have a kiss. I'd make you . . ."

Izzi and others like him were to be my companions from now on. My life had begun with abandonment—from a castle, like as not. It might end in a castle prison. As a babe I'd been thrust out. Now I was being kept in.

I started a new melody in my mind, the song of a river, coursing down from Mount Ormallo, overflowing its banks, racing where it would, carrying away sheep and houses and people. No prison for this river. It was free free free.

After a while, exhausted by rage and fear, I fell asleep. I woke with a start and an idea, an ogreish, persuasive idea.

I was gagged, so I couldn't sing, but I could hum. I began to hum the Sweet Sleep Lullaby, which every Ayorthaian mother sings to every Ayorthaian babe.

"Singing to please me, are you, sweet?"

I hummed and worked my wrists behind my back, trying to stretch the rope that bound them.

"It's that ogre blood, I warrant. Does your hearers no good. Does them . . ." Izzi continued to talk. My wrists burned. I kept humming.

It seemed to take hours, but I freed my hands. Unfortunately Izzi was still awake. He even sang along with my humming.

> "Wrap your toes in moss,
>   drape your calves in velvet,
>   smile at your dimpled knees.
>
> "Sweet sleep,
>   pale moth
>   flutters by."

I slowed my humming and made my voice as honeyed and resonant as I could. Sleep, Izzi, sleep. You are in your mother's womb, and her voice surrounds you.

Let me do this, I prayed, before the guard changes and they discover that my hands are free.

Izzi hummed along for an endless while, but then his head nodded. Soon he was asleep and snoring. Victory for the ogre.

I untied my gag and pressed against the upper left corner of the cage door, where I'd felt the weakness. There it was again. The pin was halfway out of the hinge. Could I pull it out?

My transformation had made my fingers thin enough to

slip between the iron bars. I reached the pin with my thumb and forefinger, but it was greasy and I couldn't get a firm grip. I tried to grasp it with the gag. However, the cloth did nothing to improve my hold. Frustrated, I let it go, and it fell outside the cage.

The bottom of the cage was dirty and gritty. Still humming, I rubbed my hands in the filth, hoping to absorb the grease. I tried again to draw the pin out, but again my fingers slipped off. I pulled once more and was able to grip it, but it didn't come. I pulled again and again.

I wondered how much time I had.

At last I felt the pin move. I yanked, and it came out in my hand.

I pushed against the cage door and it gave, spreading wide enough to allow my arm through. I could almost reach the bolt that opened the door, but not quite.

I sat on my haunches, considering. My humming was automatic now.

The cage's lower hinge was intact. The cage walls were impenetrable. There was nothing but the bolt. I strained, and felt the cloth in my armpit tear. I strained more. The metal corner pressed into me.

I touched the bolt!

I clenched my teeth and stre-e-e-tched. I felt heat. I knew I was bleeding, but I pushed the bolt and it moved. The lock scraped open with a whine and a creak.

Izzi continued to snore.

I tottered out of the cage. At last.

I raised my arm. The cut was trifling. I picked up my gag and the rope that had tied my hands. Then I circled around Izzi to gag him and tie him up.

But why gag him? Who would hear his shouts? Perhaps I should just grab his arms and push him into a cell. I took a deep breath. My heart was pounding wildly.

He mumbled something in his sleep.

I let the breath out. Why not leave him asleep?

I grinned. If I left Izzi asleep, they wouldn't know how I'd gotten out. They might think it magic.

But would he stay asleep when I was no longer humming? I lowered my voice and readied myself.

His head lolled to the side.

I stopped humming.

Izzi slept on.

I took a lamp from its sconce. My hand trembled so, the light wavered. I pulled the door open.

A guard faced me, holding a lantern and a knife.

CHAPTER TWENTY-SEVEN

H E LOOKED ASTONISHED to see me, too. He fell back a step. I surged forward. He blocked my way and put a finger to his lips. I recognized him. He was Uju, Ivi's favorite guard.

"Come," he whispered. "I have horses saddled." He eased the dungeon door closed.

I thought of charging past him. I didn't know why he would help me. It might be a trap, but why trap me? I was believed to be in a prison cell.

I needed help. I hadn't thought beyond the dungeon. I followed Uju through the tunnel. At the turn, instead of continuing toward the Great Hall, he veered right. After a few yards we ascended half a flight of wooden steps to a door, which opened smoothly, as though in frequent use.

We entered a storage cellar and walked down a narrow aisle lined with casks of sesame-seed oil. The casks gave way to crates. I smelled tarragon. I heard a chirp, then another, then a trill. Some birds had found refuge here.

We passed through another doorway into a room of furniture shrouded in canvas. Uju crossed to a door. He threw it open, and we stepped into the gray world before dawn.

He stared at me, then whispered, "You're so comely."

Don't waste time!

The lists were on my right, the stables straight ahead, across an exercise yard where two horses waited. I mounted a dun-colored stallion, he a piebald mare. Instead of riding past the guardhouse and over the drawbridge, we crossed the moat, which was low and gave the horses no trouble.

I looked back at Ontio Castle. It hadn't been my home for very long.

The air was warm and moist. I refused to think, and I held sorrow and rage at bay. I smelled the grass in the field we cantered through, felt the soft wind on my face, heard the birds wake up, and admired the grace of my hands on the reins and the shapeliness of my knees through my skirts.

After an hour of hard riding, we reached the foothills of Mount Ormallo. We rode in the waters of a stream to confound pursuit. From there we entered a ravine, where Uju said we would spend the day.

He tethered the horses to a poplar. I sat, leaning against the ravine wall, where I was least likely to be seen from above. Uju sat near the ravine wall, too, several yards away.

I rose and went to him. "Why did you come for me?"

I'd never seen him anything but quiet and stern, and he remained so. He took more than a minute to answer me. Then he shrugged. "Her Majesty commanded me to."

Ivi! I retreated to my spot against the ravine wall.

"Where are you taking me?"

He shrugged again. "Far—" A listening look came over him.

I heard hoofbeats and the baying of a hound. Our horses! They'd see the horses!

The hoofbeats receded. I began to breathe again.

Why had Ivi sent Uju to me? Might Skulni have persuaded her to rescue me? It was possible. I hadn't learned what he could do or what his designs were.

More likely she'd wanted my beauty as far from her as could be.

The day wore on. At dusk Uju went to his saddlebags and produced a thick slice of bread and sausage for each of us. When the sky was dark, we left the ravine. Uju headed north and east, keeping to the Ormallo range. The Featherbed was north of the castle, too, but far to the west.

I couldn't go home. They'd look for me there. I had no home.

The wall I'd built around my feelings crumbled. I wept as we rode. A song rang through my mind.

> *I rode all day.*
> *I cried all night.*
> *The moon didn't glow.*
> *The stars didn't rise.*
> *A comet blazed*
> *Between my eyes.*
> *West and south,*
> *Wind and rain.*
> *Every way is*
> *Just the same.*
> *Pray give me a box*
> *To hide inside.*
> *Pray give me a spade*
> *To dig my grave.*

We passed the next day in a shallow cave and rode again through the night. At dawn we entered a landscape even more strewn with rocks and boulders than Mount Ormallo. We were riding along a narrow path on the edge of a mountain when Uju swerved behind a boulder. I followed. He slid off his mount and pulled me off mine. He clamped his hand over my mouth.

He was going to kill me!

I struggled. Then I heard loud footfalls, labored breathing.

Ivi's guards!

Why were they on foot?

I heard an angry voice and an angry answer—but not in Ayorthaian. Uju's eyes were bulging in terror.

"ROOjiNN sesh."

"MyNN eMMong aiSS."

Ogres!

Uju crept to the boulder. He waved me back, but I followed. I lay flat and peered over the rim of the path.

They came around a low tree and into view about fifteen yards below us. There were four of them, bigger than I ever was. One was female, the others male.

Their path forked only a few feet ahead of them. If they took the right-hand fork, and if the wind was in our favor, perhaps they would go on their way none the wiser.

They took the right-hand fork. Uju and I grinned at each other. I'd never seen a happier face than his.

The ogres continued up the mountain, arguing and joking. Their laughter was half snort, half bray. Were they my cousins? If they'd met me in my old form, would they have eaten me or embraced me?

I saw a red ribbon in the female's matted hair. Had it

belonged to one of her meals?

Uju's mare neighed.

"UFF vahlwa!"

Uju and I scrambled back from the path. He pulled out his dagger. *Run!* he mouthed at me. I saw him prepare to attack.

He'd die! They'd *persuade* him before he could strike.

I illused a whinny, coming from the other side of the ogres, somewhere down the mountain.

Uju turned toward me.

"AflOOn vahlwan!"

I illused an answering whinny, also down the mountain.

The ogres babbled and squabbled. I wished I could see what they were doing.

I got my wish. A head rose above the ledge.

CHAPTER TWENTY-EIGHT

*U*JU HURLED HIS dagger into the creature's throat. I caught the ogre before he could fall back among his pack. Uju and I hauled him onto the path.

We peeked back out.

An ogre looked up in our direction. "InJJ? SshrEE shAA vahlwa?" The ogre took a step toward us.

I whinnied again, but he didn't turn. I had to distract them.

I whispered to Uju, "Fill your mind with song."

He nodded.

I illused a woman's voice from the direction of the whinnies. "Did you hear something, Ollo?" it said. Then I filled my mind with song.

Below us the ogre stopped and grinned. I saw his mouth form the Ayorthaian word for *friend*.

I illused a male voice, singing, "I heard it, too. 'Friend,' it said."

Would they come after their companion or seek their prey?

They headed down the mountain.

Uju grabbed my arm. We started picking our way upward, taking care to be quiet.

We climbed for ten minutes or more. I fought an urge to stop my silent singing and listen to hear if they were close. Too dangerous—if they were still persuading, I'd hear them.

Uju turned, a rapt smile on his face. He began to pull me back down the mountain.

He'd listened to the ogres! I fought him. I managed to jam my hands against his ears.

I saw comprehension return. We hurried up the mountain again. I hoped he had a destination in mind.

He did. We reached it shortly, a rock-strewn ridge with a view into the valley. We could see the path we'd been on. There were our horses, still behind the boulder. There were the ogres, not far below the place we'd first seen them, trudging back up the mountain.

One veered aside and found our horses and their dead comrade. They began to climb toward us, pointing out our tracks as they came.

Uju started kicking stones down the mountain, hefting rocks and throwing them. I became a throwing zealot. Between us we hurled a huge, half-buried rock. I heaved and tossed and pitched the heaviest rocks I could lift, never stopping to see the result.

Then Uju was pulling me away. We stumbled back as half the mountain below gave way and buried the ogres and our unfortunate horses.

We scrambled down the far side of the ridge. I hoped the ground beneath us wouldn't collapse. At the bottom, Uju started climbing the adjacent slope.

"Wait!" I cried. I had to stop to catch my breath.

"Not safe. Come!"

I followed, holding my side and panting. What would we do without horses?

Finally he collapsed, halfway up. I collapsed next to him. After he stopped panting, he said, "You saved us both."

"*You* saved us both."

"Queen Ivi told me to kill you."

Could she hate me so much? Could she be so wicked?

"Not in so many words, but her meaning was clear enough." Fright had loosened his tongue. "She said you were half ogre. She said we'd all be safer without you. I was going to kill you, but you'd grown so beautiful, I stopped believing her."

Beauty had saved me.

"But if I had killed you, the ogres would have killed me." He smiled ruefully. "If I was dead, she wouldn't be able to knight me."

She'd promised to elevate him, just as she'd elevated me.

"I'll tell everyone I found you dead, but I'll tell her I killed you. I want a scrap of your gown to prove you're dead. She'll knight me yet."

"Of course." I tore a bit from the hem. My beautiful new gown was creased and filthy.

"I'll bloody it up somehow."

Faugh! "Are you going to leave me here?" If he was, he might as well kill me. I'd be dead soon enough, with no food and no idea where water might be.

"No, Milady. I won't abandon you." He shrugged. "We'll be there before we die of hunger or thirst."

"Be where?"

"Gnome Caverns. The gnomes may take you in. If they do, you'll be safe—if you can stay down there."

zhamM's prediction was coming true.

Uju found a cave for us to rest in. I was exhausted, but I couldn't sleep. The sun was still high and hot when he said we should leave.

"Anyone can see us." I had never felt more visible, not even when I was ugly and twenty people were staring at me.

He shrugged. "Nonetheless." He had returned to taciturnity.

I trudged after him. The heel came off my right slipper. "Uju?"

He shrugged, so I knew he was listening.

"When you reach home, would you tell Prince Ijori that one of my cousins ate me?"

He nodded. Good.

Rock walls rose around us, forming serpentine pathways. It was a landscape to be lost in forever. But Uju never hesitated, choosing each new chasm as if he was following a rope.

The day wore on. My tongue felt gritty and dusty. Visions of iced ostumo, mead, raspberry juice, took over my imagination. I was parched enough to long even for apple juice.

Uju turned a corner. I followed and then stopped short. He had opened a rock door into the cliff.

The doorway was lower than my height and wider than my girth. Uju ducked and entered. I hung back, thinking of the castle dungeon.

But the air that wafted out of the tunnel was cool and fresh. The floor was carpeted. The pattern was of pink pails and pink hammers and pink chisels on a light-green background.

How could I fear? I hunched over and entered.

The light dimmed. Uju had closed the door, soundlessly. I turned. The door was indistinguishable from the surrounding rock. When would I see the sun again?

The tunnel was brighter than torchlight. The wall on my right seemed to be crisscrossed by sparkling veins and arteries. I guessed this was the glow iron zhamM had mentioned. It was magical—gnomish magic.

The tunnel wound steeply down. We heard gurgling but saw not a drop of water. I was certain we were nearing the center of the world.

Below us, the tunnel ended in a small circular room where a gnome sat, reading a book.

Uju called out, ".fwthchor evtoogh drzzay eerth ymmadboech evtoogh drzzaY"

The gnome, a female, looked up. She marked her place in her book, pushed back her chair, and exited through the rock where she was standing. Through the rock! She seemed to melt into it and was gone. More gnomish magic.

"!ghufzO" Uju cried. He raced to where she'd been and pounded on the rock wall.

I joined him and stared at the spot where she had vanished. It looked no different from the rest of the rock wall— smooth, glistening, coral colored. Uju kicked it.

"What did you say to her?"

He slumped into her chair. "It was a greeting."

I wasn't worried. I had zhamM's prediction to rely on. I was to see him in Gnome Caverns.

"We can go back," I said, "and find another entrance." I'd heard there were many. But it would be a long climb, especially without food or water.

He didn't stand up.

"Why can't we?"

"It was an entrance."

Yes?

Then I understood. It was an entrance only, not an exit. We wouldn't be able to find the door. We were stuck here.

I still wasn't concerned. "We'll get in. A gnome once predicted I'd see him in Gnome Caverns."

Uju laughed bitterly. "A gnome predicted I'd be given a centaur before my thirty-second birthday. That birthday passed eleven years ago."

Oh. I sank to the floor. It might end here, then. We'd die of thirst with water gurgling somewhere nearby. Idly I opened the gnome's book. Naturally the words were Gnomic, punctuated and capitalized backward as the gnomes did.

If only I could get to that gurgling water! I wondered how it could sound so close with solid rock between us and it. The rock must capture the sound somehow. The rock *was* solid. Uju had pounded on it and kicked it.

But she'd passed through it. Perhaps . . .

"Uju, stand up!"

He stood slowly.

"Step aside!"

He did.

I went to the wall and touched it lightly. It felt soft as gossamer. My finger went into it, as if it were fog. I smacked the wall. Solid rock. I approached it gently again, and my hand went right in.

I turned to him. "We can go through."

"What if it seizes up around us?"

Then we'd die in the rock rather than outside it. "The secret seems to be to move smoothly."

A dozen gnomish warriors might be waiting on the other side, pointing their swords at us.

"I'm going to try it," I said. I thought, Glide, and stepped into the wall.

It felt like stepping through feathers. Then I was out.

A moment later Uju came through. "You saved me again."

We were in the same tunnel. The wall we'd gone through was filmy from this side. I could see the glow iron sparkling on the far wall.

I looked for the source of the gurgling. There it was. Just past the edge of the carpeting was a trough through which water streamed.

No one was in sight. Uju and I threw ourselves down. I cupped my hands and drank. I heard Uju slurping next to me.

The water tasted pure and sweet. I thought I'd never get enough.

"Maid Aza? Maid azacH? You came through our curtain!"

The voice was mild and breathy. I scrambled up and curtsied. "Master zhamM!"

CHAPTER TWENTY-NINE

N EXT TO ME, Uju bowed.

The green gentleman, in a yellow paisley tunic with emerald buttons, bowed in return. "Maid azacH," he said, straightening, "you are changed, just as you'd hoped. You are smaller, and there is almost no htun in your hair. I've regretted your absence from the Featherbed." He sang,

> *"I'm not a Sir, I'm a serf,*
> *And my enemy's worse*
> *Than a knight ever cursed."*

He remembered my words! And the tune, more or less.

"I've missed your voice. I'm glad it's here." He smiled. "And you've come with it, to be exact."

I recalled his sense of humor. If he'd missed me, perhaps he'd let me stay.

"Thank you, Sir," he told Uju, "for bringing Maid azacH."

I introduced them, and they both bowed again.

Uju sang, "I'm not a Sir, I'm a guard."

zhamM and I both smiled at the joke, the first I'd heard Uju make.

zhamM explained that the woman who'd fled from us had done so because Uju had misspoken the gnomes' traditional greeting, "Digging is good for the wealth and for the health." Instead, he'd said that *killing* was good for both.

She had thought the mistake innocent but hadn't wanted to stay, just in case. So she'd fetched zhamM, who'd talked often of his expected visitor.

"Come," he said. "We'll see if the gnomes can equal the Featherbed in hospitality."

He turned out to be an aristocrat and a judge, a widyeH in Gnomic, a gnome of honor. Servants came and led Uju and me away. zhamM promised to have a meal ready for us when we returned from our baths.

I was taken to the bath caverns for female gnomes. There was a mirror in the alcove where I was to disrobe. I was dirtier than I'd ever been, but the potion hadn't worn off.

Naked, I stepped to the edge of an underground lake. Lanterns bobbed in tiny boats. Gnome ladies swam or reclined on rocky islets, or paddled about in bubbling springs. We were all naked, but because of their wrinkled leathery skin, they didn't seem so—as a lizard or a snake doesn't.

No one was staring, but I waded in quickly, submerging myself as soon as the water was deep enough. It was pleasantly warm, and it lapped against me in a soothing rhythm.

I smelled sulfur, the gnomes' favorite scent. At the Featherbed their rooms always smelled of it by the time they left.

The lake went on as far as I could see, branching into smaller caverns. The surrounding rock was pink and ivory and wet, like the inside of an enormous mouth. I wondered how sound would carry. If I'd been alone, I would have yodeled.

I swam through sea foam, which turned out to be soap bubbles, coming from a spring below me. I raised my arm and found bubbles clinging to it. Scrub brushes were on the closest lantern boat. It was glorious to become clean. The soap-bubble water was buoyant. I didn't have to paddle to stay afloat, and the mud I shed disappeared in a trice. I gave myself over to the sensation of the water on my skin, the pleasure of massaging my scalp, the vividness of the brush on my back.

I sang a toddler's bath song.

> *"Sudsy bubbles float*
> *Past a bath-toy boat.*
> *Slip slide slither soap*
> *Up and down the belly slope.*
> *Out peeks the knee,*
> *Out peep the feet."*

When not a speck of dirt remained, I swam away from the soap spring and floated on my back, drifting. I fell asleep and woke only when I passed through a stretch of pulsing, tingly water. My hunger returned in force. I swam to shore.

My filthy gown was gone. I found instead a female gnome's robe and undergarments, freshly washed and smelling sulfuric. The robe was a golden color. I suspected that the threads were actual gold, although they were soft as silk. The fabric would have fascinated Ivi.

The neckline was square in front and rounded at the back. The shoulders were too broad, and the waist was vastly too big, but there was a sash, which improved matters. The skirt would have been too short, but a border of more gold cloth had been sewn on.

I considered myself in the mirror. The bodice hung loose. The shoulders bunched up. However, I was still beautiful. I was radiant—among the gnomes, who thought me as hideous as I'd ever been.

A servant conducted me to an alcove, where Uju and zhamM sat at a round table. Uju was attired in gnome finery too. zhamM may have supplied the tunic, because it had emerald buttons.

Uju kept looking uneasily at the rock walls. I wondered what was troubling him.

Servants appeared bearing steaming platters. I remember little of the meal. I was too exhausted. I know we were served root vegetables and there was conversation, but I have no memory of what was said. I don't remember finishing my food or being taken to a bedchamber.

When I awoke, the room was dark. I didn't know where I was. After a few moments I remembered. Oh, yes. Gnome Caverns. I was an exile.

I wondered what was taking place in Ayortha. Was Ijori still shuddering over the memory of our kiss? Was Skulni carrying out his plans, whatever they were? Did Mother and Father know of my disgrace yet? Was the search for me still underway? Might they pursue me here?

Would the gnomes let me stay?

I sang to quiet my thoughts:

> *"Climb the day.*
> *Drop your dreams.*
> *Possess the day."*

I wondered if it was morning.

I sat up and saw the glowing outline of a door. I slid sideways, and sideways, and sideways. I finally reached the edge of the bed and started cautiously for the door, hoping not to trip over anything.

When I opened it, a servant bustled in with a lantern. "!evtoogh fwthchoR" she said gaily.

"!eftook swithcoR" I said, trying to get it right.

She giggled and lit a lamp. I saw my bedchamber. Its walls were hammered copper laid over the underlying rock. Here and there a triangle or a square or a diamond shape had been painted on the copper in bright blue or green or red. The effect was cheery.

The entire chamber had a lighthearted charm. There was a yellow rocking chair, a pink bureau, and a blue-and-white table. Atop the bureau was a bowl of colored stones— amber, blue, violet. I wondered if they were pebbles or gems.

There was no fireplace. It always seemed comfortably cool down here.

The maid said slowly and carefully, "Dress you. After I you widyeH zhamM take." She curtsied and left the room.

Another gnome's gown had been spread out on an easy chair. After I dressed, the maid led me through a maze of carpeted tunnel to an open door.

I entered a cozy parlor. There were four wide easy chairs, upholstered in bright fabrics, each with a matching footstool and a side table. The legs of the tables, chairs, and footstools were set with stones. On each table was a bowl of pebbles, or gems, like the one in my chamber. A low table was heaped with books. A circular hooked rug extended almost to the cavern walls. The walls were alive with glow iron, making the chamber as bright as could be without sunlight.

zhamM came in through a door across the room. "Good morning, Maid azacH."

It was morning then. "Good morning, widyeH zhamM."

"Oh! My title." He led me to a chair. "They are bringing breakfast."

"I'm the chambermaid. I should be waiting on you."

"Not here. Here you are my guest."

Breakfast arrived on a tray: raw carrots, carrot puree, and glistening candied carrots. To the side was a tumbler of orange liquid. There were also two cups and a silver ostumo pot.

zhamM said he'd eaten earlier. He indicated my meal. "Carrots done three ways and carrot juice and ostumo. We gnomes have come to enjoy your ostumo. It is a delicacy, to be exact."

I poured the ostumo for both of us. The color was right,

but the smell was sharp. He sipped his and looked satisfied. I sipped mine and began to cough.

He put down his cup. "I see we haven't got it right yet. The carrot juice will be excellent, however."

It was, and the other carrot preparations were tasty, too. I felt guilty for wishing for a muffin.

"Where is Uju?"

"He set out for Ontio at dawn. He said he disliked being underground. Do you mind it?"

I shook my head. I didn't mind at all. This was nothing like the dungeon at Ontio.

"Good. Few humans are able to remain here as long as you already have."

Did this mean I could stay? "It's cozy."

"That is how we feel. But Guard Uju wouldn't even wait for you to awaken. We gave him a centaur to ride when he left."

"The prediction!" I said.

"Yes. The gnome who made it must have been thinking of Guard Uju's age in gnome years."

"Oh."

"Before leaving, he promised to convince your pursuers of your death."

Good.

But word would reach Mother and Father. "widyeH

zhamM, would someone be able to deliver a letter to my parents?"

He inclined his head. "I'll see to it."

After I finished eating, he said, "You are in danger, as I foresaw. Tell me what brought you here. Perhaps a gnome can help."

No one could help. I didn't want to talk about it, but I owed zhamM an explanation, and the gnomes needed to know I was an outlaw.

"What took you to Ontio Castle in the first place?"

"The royal wedding." I told him everything— about the ceremony, the composing game with Ijori, meeting Ivi, the centaurs.

He listened quietly, now and then sipping the bitter ostumo.

I wept over King Oscaro. zhamM gave me his handkerchief, which was embroidered with green thread. Then he took another handkerchief from another pocket and shed a tear, too. He rang for a servant, and when one came, he told her to bring a pitcher of water.

The water arrived, and I continued my tale. zhamM kept my glass full. When I told about illusing for Ivi, he asked me to demonstrate.

I illused Uju's voice coming from the air above one of the chairs. The voice sang lines from a traveling song.

"The hills rise and fall,
worn up and down by foreign feet.
Signs of home abound:
the sky, the weeds . . ."

"Superb!" zhamM said. "How is it done?"

I explained. "No one else can do it," I added. "Perhaps my birth family would be able to."

"The innkeepers are not your true parents?"

I thought everyone who visited the Featherbed knew. "They're my true parents, but not my birth parents."

"I see. Now let me try this illusing." He tried and failed and tried again. He said, "I have it now," and failed again. He tried twice more, and then his voice came from somewhere over the low table. "Marvelous, to be exact," it said. He clapped his hands.

How could he illuse, when Mother and Sir Uellu, the best singers I knew, had failed?

"Thank you for showing me, Maid azacH." This came from the ceiling.

He couldn't imitate other voices or sounds, but he could illuse.

"Please continue with your tale," he illused from near the door.

I suspected he might never again speak without illusing.

I went on. He looked shocked when I told of Ivi's threats against me. But he laughed over my beauty-spell calamity and asked to see my marble toe.

After I assured him that it didn't hurt, he said he wouldn't mind a glow-iron toe.

I continued my tale. I mentioned my friendship with Ijori and said that he'd kissed me, but I told it in as offhand a manner as I could.

I broke down again when I reached my final night at the castle. I had to wait before I could relate Sir Uellu's accusations against me and Ivi's lies.

"Then they tied my hands and gagged me. widyeH zhamM, it's terrible for a singer to be gagged." I finished the tale, feeling tired enough for another night's sleep.

He was silent, his hands folded in his lap, his head bent. Such a sympathetic silence it was. It took in my grief and misery and didn't try to put a bright face on what had happened.

After a few minutes he reached into the bowl of pebbles on the table next to him and selected a largish stone about the size of his thumb. He came to my chair and showed it to me. "What do you see?"

"A rock?"

"What color is it?"

"Dull black."

He put his free hand on mine. "Now what color is it?"

"Oh!" It wasn't black at all. It was another dark color, but not a color I knew. I had no words to describe its hue, but I felt it, an intensity behind my eyes that was almost pain.

He let my hand go, and the rock became dull black again. He returned it to the bowl and sat back down. "That rock was htun. Most humans can't see htun, even if I hold their hands. Maid azacH, I doubt you have a single drop of ogre blood in you. However, my dear cousin, I am certain that one of your ancestors was a gnome."

CHAPTER THIRTY

I, PART GNOME?

"These are my reasons," zhamM said. "Your hair has htun highlights, which no other human hair has. It used to be all htun before you drank that dreadful potion. I must say, you were foolhardy when you did so."

"But—"

He held up a hand. "You were foolhardy." He smiled at me. ".byjadh heemyeh odh ubaech achoedzaY Foolishness may have golden offspring. I hope yours does."

I did too.

"There are more reasons than your hair to think you are part gnome. Before drinking the potion, you were wider than most humans. You were taller as well, which we cannot take credit for. However, we can take credit for your thinking it's cozy here.

"What's more, you discovered how to penetrate our

rock curtain when you arrived. To be exact, no human has ever done so before. And I can illuse, although I am no singer."

"But . . . but Sir Uellu said I wormed my way into people's affections as an ogre would. He said I looked like an ogre, too."

"Yes. I'm very put out with him." He hesitated. "Maid azacH, are you sorry to be part gnome?"

"No!" Although gnomes were ugly by human standards, their ugliness was far less repugnant than an ogre's—not repugnant at all, really. It was the difference, perhaps, between the looks of a cockroach and a grasshopper.

Besides, the gnomes who'd stayed at the Featherbed had always been kind. Mother and Father had liked them, too. "I'm not sorry—if I really am part gnome."

"You are. It has happened before. My aunt's husband had some human in him."

Now was the time to ask. "widyeH zhamM, may I stay here?"

"Cousin, did you think we would toss you out?"

I wept again. For the second time in my life I was being accepted into a fold.

zhamM cleared his throat. "Perhaps you can teach us to make ostumo as it should be made."

I laughed through my tears. "I'll be glad to."

He cleared his throat again. "To be exact, you can do more than that for us."

I wiped my eyes. "Yes?"

"We would love to hear you sing. I have spoken of your voice ever since I first heard it. But also, I know of no human songs about us, so . . . would you compose a few?"

I wrote a letter to Mother and Father, telling all. zhamM gave it to a messenger and also dispatched two gnome armorers to Ontio Castle. While displaying their newest swords and shields, the armorers would see how news of my death had been received and whether Ivi retained her former power.

"You may stay here as long as you like, Maid azacH," zhamM said. "But it's best to know where matters stand."

I wanted to ask the armorers to take note of Ijori—if he seemed to mourn me or if he seemed untroubled. But then I remembered I didn't care.

I wrote a series of songs about living with the gnomes. The song making saved me from despondency and anguish. I couldn't think of Ivi or Ijori without rage or pain. Writing songs was better.

My first song was about zhamM and what he meant to me. I sang it at a dinner in the Banquet Hall. I was hardly nervous. Compared with my feelings the first time I sang at the castle, I was as calm as a tree. zhamM had promised that everyone would love my singing, and I believed him.

As I sang, I discovered how gnomes blush—the tip of zhamM's bulbous nose turned violet.

> "widyeH zhamM, the green gentleman,
> to be exact, came many times
> to our inn. He said my hair
> was htun, and htun, he said,
> was beautiful. I was ugly,
> he said I was. I knew I was.
> He called all humans ugly, to be
> exact. I was uglier
> than the rest, but he thought not.
> The green gentleman thought not.
>
> "If I leave here ever,
> if I come back never,
> I will know that there is htun,
> and it is beautiful.
> Beautiful, to be exact.
>
> "widyeH zhamM, the green gentleman,
> to be exact, saw I'd come,
> danger on my shoulder. He didn't

> *call me cousin then. Pebbles here*
> *are worth coaches home. Footstools*
> *are worth castles. Castles, to be exact.*
> *Today, the green gentleman called*
> *me cousin. I can't see*
> *htun without his hand. But*
> *he called me cousin. Cousin,*
> *to be exact.*

> *"If I leave here ever,*
> *if I come back never,*
> *I will know that there is zhamM*
> *and he is priceless. Priceless,*
> *to be exact."*

My next song described the magnificence of Gnome Caverns. At the entrance to the Banquet Hall, for example, a milky rock tower rose, perhaps fifteen times my height. In clusters around the chamber were delicate rock straws that extended, thinner than my pinkie, from floor to ceiling.

The only aspect of the Banquet Hall I omitted from my song was the food. I yearned for more variety than what is dug up from the ground. After a week I would have given my golden plate for a leg of chicken, a scone, a bowl of fruit. zhamM knew, I think, and others might have, too. Often I'd pick at my food and remind myself I had to eat to stay alive.

The greatest marvel in Gnome Caverns was the gnomes. They accepted my presence as though I had lived among them forever. They told me over and again—in pantomime, since few spoke Ayorthaian—how glad they were to have a human visitor. They stayed in our world sometimes, but we never stayed in theirs.

They loved my voice and my songs, which zhamM translated. They swayed, just as we did, when they liked something. And they liked everything!

Two weeks after I came, a gnome asked me to sing for her daughter, who was to begin her apprenticeship as a jeweler. There was to be a ceremony. Both of them would be honored if I sang, and the mother would pay me. Would a small diamond be enough?

A diamond! There were no coins here. The currency was gems. I'd never been paid for a song before. I would have refused the jewel, but zhamM told me to accept. Then he educated me about gnome apprenticeships so I could write the song.

The ceremony took place in the market cavern. The maid chanted something to her new master and bowed from her waist. The maid's mother gave the master a scroll. I was told it was time to sing. Everyone smiled.

This was my song:

"Today we celebrate."

They began to sway.

> *"Today you end*
> *and you begin. The old*
> *is still sweeter*
> *than the new. You*
> *notice everything.*
> *Your shoe has a scuff.*
> *Your master hunches over.*
> *Your fingers don't do*
> *as they're told. But*
> *already you can pick*
> *a stone. You've*
> *loved the bead bowl*
> *since you were six.*
> *Remember?*
> *Remember, and*
> *don't forget*
> *the moments*
> *of your beginning.*
> *Name your tools.*
> *Name your bench.*
> *Name your lantern.*

"Let us sing!

Let us sway!

Let us eat and drink!

What a jeweler you'll be!

We'll buy your wares!

We'll be lucky to know you!

We're lucky to know you now."

At the end they raised their hands, as we do. Then the maid's father passed out tumblers of mineral water, the gnomes' favorite drink, as ostumo was ours. We all drank, and the proceedings ended.

The mother paid me. The diamond was smaller than the ones in the pebble bowl in my bed cavern. But it was mine. I'd never thought I'd own a diamond.

As zhamM and I left the market cavern, a candle vendor wanted to sell me candles. An old woman wanted to sell me tree-root confections, awful shriveled stuff. They knew I had a diamond to spend.

When we reached zhamM's parlor, I asked him to look into the future once more for me. I was wondering if I ever might go home.

He straightened a book on his low table, then rang for a servant. It was time for his afternoon ostumo. I had spent hours in the gnomes' kitchen, going over the process of making ostumo, and the gnomish chefs could now produce a drinkable brew.

He picked up a book, then set it down. "I have already looked ahead again for you. Maid azacH . . . when I foretold for you at the Featherbed, I saw you here, but I didn't see beyond. Here you are, and we have gone beyond."

He was frightening me.

"There may be a beyond that follows what I saw this time."

"What did you see?"

"I saw you lying on the ground."

Dead?

"Several figures milled about. Remorse and gloating came from one of them. Remorse and gloating, both at once, to be exact."

"Was I dead?"

"I don't know. You didn't stir."

CHAPTER THIRTY-ONE

I ASKED ZHAMM if the people surrounding me were gnomes.

"They must have been. You were somewhere in Gnome Caverns. I saw glow iron again."

"Was I much older than I am now?" Perhaps he'd seen years into the future.

"I couldn't tell. It could be tomorrow or ten years hence."

"Must it happen?"

"No. You could come to a crossroad and choose a different direction. Or the figure gloating over you might."

"But the likelihood is that it will come to pass, yes?"

zhamM nodded. "Yes, to be exact."

"What should I do?"

"Be cautious. When you have a decision to make, consider carefully. Violence is rare here, but a gnome is an implacable enemy."

If I departed Gnome Caverns and never returned, I'd be safe from zhamM's prediction. I thought it over in bed that night and decided to remain at least until the armorers returned from Ontio Castle. Their news would help me choose how to proceed.

The next day the messenger arrived from the Featherbed with a letter from Mother and Father. I took it to my bed cavern to read. When I opened it, I found a note from Ijori tucked inside.

Ijori! At the Featherbed? My heart skipped, then beat too fast.

I read his first.

> *Dear heart,*
>
> *I write in fear that you will never read my words, that evil—more evil—has befallen you and you are beyond the reach of my love.*
>
> *I have given this note to your good parents in case you come here—although you mustn't stay with them. If you do, you will certainly be discovered.*
>
> *In the queen's apartments after the Sing I was too angry for clear thought. But in the night that followed, I grew certain that you told the truth. I know the queen. It is far more*

253

likely that she threatened you than that you conived for position and power. Indeed, it is more likely for the sun to turn blue than for you to be a schemer. Please forgive my mistrust. If you don't, I'll never forgive myself.

However, I still wish you'd confided in me. We would have found a way out together.

I hope the change in your appearance was not forced on you, too. Paradoxically, I also hope you didn't choose it. I never thought you ugly. I should have told you long ago. No one has eyes like yours. Or an aroma like yours. I loved the size of you from the first.

I am searching for you. I sing of you as I search. You are my love. I hope someday to be yours once again.

> *Your penitent*
> *Ijori*

I forgave him. Of course I forgave him. He needn't repent.

Now that I was beautiful, I didn't want to believe he'd never thought me ugly. But perhaps it was true. He was extraordinary.

I wondered if we'd ever be together again. I was likely to

die here, but at least he wouldn't think I was already dead. If he was away searching for me, he wouldn't hear Uju's tale of my death.

I opened Mother and Father's letter. Mother wrote that guards had come. They had searched the inn while the guests stood outside in a rainstorm. Afterward the guards had questioned everyone.

> *They wanted to know if we'd seen any ogre-
> ish tendencies in you. We said absolutely not.
> Father sang five verses of your virtues. Yarry
> and Ollo and I trotted out all our old songs
> to you and yours to us, whether those guards
> wanted to hear them or not.*

I started to cry.

The letter went on: "We were told that land won't come to us after all, but that Ayortha will pay for the new roof and the new wing."

As Ijori had promised, the crown had been generous.

> *At first we doubted who would stay in the
> new wing or under the new roof. Half our
> guests decamped immediately after the guards
> did. But then the prince and his dog came, and*

the half who stayed were thrilled. The prince saved us, I'm sure. Father is fashioning a wooden sign with the date of His Highness's visit. Prince Ijori seems to think as little of the lies about you as we do. We think he is a fine young man, with a fine ear for true notes and false.

Father wishes to add a few words. I am, as always, Your Loving Mother.

He wrote,

Daughter, we didn't need your note—or a prince's visit—to tell us you'd done nothing wrong. We know the daughter we raised. We fear for your future, but never for your character. You take our love and our trust wherever you wander. Father.

I wept harder.

zhamM, out of his endless goodness, sent the messenger back into the world to find Ijori. "But be cautious in your inquiries," he instructed. "We don't want Maid azacH linked with gnomes. When you find Prince Ijori, tell him his love is well, but tell him not to come." He turned to me.

"It isn't safe until we're certain the court believes you dead."

I was eager to write a reply to Ijori, assuring him of love and forgiveness.

"Write it," zhamM said. "Say what you want him to know. But it mustn't be sent. It might fall into the wrong hands. To be exact, it might cause my prediction to come true."

I did write the note, a song.

> When you pet Oochoo,
> my dearest,
> you pause, your palm so close
> the air shivers. And then
> your hand—light as snow,
> velvet fingers—bestows
> love behind the ears,
> beneath the chin.
> You'll be king.
> I may not see it.
> You'll rule with a hand
> light as snow,
> velvet fingers,
> love beyond the throne,
> love to the borders.
> I wish you well.

zhamM promised to give Ijori the note if anything happened to me.

I received more requests for songs. I sang at celebrations of all sorts: opening a new home cavern, a betrothal, a gold strike, the repayment of a debt. In a month I half filled a purse with gems, small ones, to be exact.

I turned sixteen. I didn't tell zhamM. He would have given me gifts, and he'd given me too much already.

The armorers hadn't yet returned from Ontio Castle, but zhamM said he expected them daily. One morning he asked me if I'd like to see him at work.

I was eager to watch. In Ayortha trials were decided by panels of judges. The gnomes, however, allowed a single judge to rule on cases and dole out punishments.

Court was held in their queen's Throne Room. She wasn't present, and I'd never seen her. zhamM said she was elderly and rarely left her bed.

Two rows of benches had been set up, with an aisle down the middle. zhamM sat in a high-backed silver chair facing the benches. He donned a jeweled cap with two bills, turning the cap so the bills were above his ears. I sat at the end of the first bench. A dozen gnomes—men, women, and three children—came in and sat near me. A minute later a solitary male gnome entered and chose a bench on the other side of the aisle.

zhamM said, "Who has the complaint?"

The man seated next to me said, "I do, widyeH zhamM. I am logH. rigK stole my shovel."

rigK denied stealing anything. The other gnomes described the circumstances surrounding the theft. I believed them.

At the end, zhamM turned his cap around so the bills pointed front and back. He closed his eyes. People began to chat. rigK took a lanyard out of the pocket of his tunic and began to work on it.

After a full ten minutes, zhamM opened his eyes. "This is my judgment: rigK, I am convinced you stole the shovel. You may keep it."

I blushed for zhamM. I'd expected wisdom from him. The other gnomes left the room without a protest.

He chuckled. "I see your face, Maid azacH. Our methods are unlike human methods. For us, a trial is a crossroad. When I turned my cap, I looked into the future. I imagined several possible rulings and what would result from them."

If only Sir Uellu had been able to look into the future before he'd accused me. He'd have seen I wouldn't harm anyone.

If only he'd looked carefully into the past.

"In this case," zhamM said, "I was reluctant to let the thief have the shovel, but in every future I imagined, the shovel's owner was better off without it, and the thief was a more honest gnome with it."

"But widyeH zhamM," I said, "stealing is wrong. Shouldn't the thief be punished regardless of what's to come?"

"Never regardless." He removed his judge's hat and stood. "In this instance, every possible punishment made this thief more likely to steal again."

I didn't approve of gnomish justice. If zhamM were to judge Ivi for her crimes, he might foresee that my future and Ayortha's future, and Ivi's future conduct as well, would be better if she weren't punished. Then he wouldn't punish her.

It made me angry even to think of. We'd suffered at her hands. I was still suffering. I wrote a ditty about the trial:

> *Who judges the judge who judges wrong?*
> *The sentence too weak,*
> *The sentence too strong.*
> *The penance too quick,*
> *The penance too long.*
> *Who judges the judge who judges wrong?*

CHAPTER THIRTY-TWO

*T*HE AFTERNOON FOLLOWING the trial, zhamM told me he would be leaving in two days. There were several trials he had to preside over beyond Gnome Caverns.

"Near the Featherbed?"

"No. In the south."

"Oh." I didn't want him to leave, although I didn't need him. Everyone was kind, and a few gnomes spoke Ayorthaian. I had been here for six weeks. I knew how to find whatever I wanted. But zhamM made me feel safe. If a crossroad came, he would recognize it and know what to do.

"I'll bring back a bushel of human food—food for humans, to be exact."

"Anything but apples."

Before he left, the armorers returned from Ontio Castle. Their most important news, wonderful news, was that the king's health had improved. He'd opened his eyes, and he followed people's movements with them. He couldn't walk or talk, but he could raise the pinky finger of his left hand. Sir Enole thought a full recovery possible.

I hugged zhamM, who looked almost as pleased as I felt.

The news that followed was mixed. The king's council was meeting openly again, and food had been dispatched to the drought-stricken south. Ivi still ruled, but nowadays she could be persuaded out of her worst notions. There continued to be occasional mutterings about rebellion.

"Have the birds returned? Are people allowed to sing?"

Yes, and yes.

"What of Maid azacH?" zhamM said. "Is she spoken of?"

The armorer named dyfF said, "You are believed dead, Maid azacH. Master Uju let it be known that you died saving him from ogres."

How kind! "Was he believed?"

"He said no one questioned his tale. I expect he whispered a different story in your queen's ear."

"You called him *Master* Uju," I said. "Not *Sir*? The queen didn't knight him?"

"No," dyfF said. "I don't think he was knighted."

"Was Maid azacH exonerated?" zhamM asked.

"There was much debate," dyfF said, "but in the end you

weren't exonerated." The tip of his nose turned violet. "You had still sung for the queen. They believe you schemed to win your position."

"Humans!" zhamM snorted.

It wasn't safe yet for me to leave Gnome Caverns.

"Did Prince Ijori return?" I said.

"No," dyfF said. "He was away the whole while."

zhamM left the next morning. We said good-bye in the Banquet Hall after breakfast. He seemed almost as unhappy as I felt.

"I feel foreboding," he said. "Be on the watch for cross-roads. If you need advice, go to dyfF. He can't see ahead, but he has a good mind for what's nearby."

zhamM said he'd be back in three weeks at the latest. "If you need me, dyfF will send a messenger. I can be back in two days."

I nodded again and sang a bit of a parting song.

> *"May the path open before you.*
> *May all your hills roll*
> *placidly up and*
> *gently down."*

He began to sway, and his worried expression faded.

> *"May the sun smile sweetly.*
> *May the rain fall softly.*
> *May a breeze ruffle your hair.*
> *May your host receive you with charm.*
> *May your rest be calm.*
> *May you be glad wherever you are."*

He raised his hands. "Farewell, Maid azacH. I wish you could illuse all the way to me wherever I go."

I wasn't likely to be bored while he was gone. I had eight songs to write in the next week, and I'd likely receive more commissions. In addition, I was studying Gnomic from a book zhamM had given me. I hoped to amaze him with my progress when he returned.

I hoped to amaze him with something else as well—a gift. I started for the market. I hadn't spent even a flake of my song fees. zhamM paid for my meals, and my bed cavern belonged to him. My wardrobe closet was full of gnomish gowns and sashes that he'd provided. He said my songs and delicious ostumo left him in my debt.

So now I wanted to buy something for him, a tunic. He loved them so. He had striped tunics and flowered tunics and paisley tunics and plaid tunics, all with emerald buttons. I knew from Father, who collected brass stirrups, that if you love a thing, one more is always welcome.

Emerald buttons were beyond my purse, but I hoped to find a tunic embroidered with htun thread that I could afford. I went to the stall of zhamM's tailor and discovered to my dismay that a dozen purses would be needed for a htun-embroidered tunic.

I had no idea what to buy instead. I wandered from stall to stall. There were jeweled shovels, jeweled hammers, and jeweled chamber pots, of all things. There was even a jeweled strongbox—which seemed to defeat the purpose of a strongbox.

A peddler proffered a tray of root candy. Icing had been applied so that each piece looked like a jewel. To me it was a case of one inedible thing being disguised as a different inedible thing.

In a stationer's stall, I saw just the thing for zhamM: a clothbound notebook. The cloth appeared a dull black. Gold thread ran through it, but there were no gems.

"?htun" I asked, pointing at it.

The vendor nodded. ".htun"

The pages were lined. I could write songs in it. If there was time, perhaps I could find someone to help me translate them into Gnomic. zhamM would love it.

"?otz ymmaD" One of the few phrases I knew. It meant, How much? I opened my purse.

The vendor took out a dozen gems. We made the exchange.

I turned away from the stall clutching my booty. I found myself facing another peddler, a gnome maiden who smiled eagerly. Along with combs and laces, her tray contained things I'd yearned for—a bun studded with pecans, a wedge of cheese, a bunch of grapes. And an apple.

"Just for you," she said in heavily accented Ayorthaian.

Was it really human food, or root candy disguised as human food? I touched the bun. It gave way, and root candy was hard. The bun had to be real.

I had reached a crossroad, but I didn't recognize it.

The peddler pulled off a grape and gave it to me. A few gnomes stopped to watch. I popped the grape into my mouth. My observers grimaced, but the grape was heaven, juicy and sweet, the best grape I'd ever eaten. The peddler pointed at my purse. I took out a diamond pebble and held it out to her. She held up two fingers.

Two diamonds for a few morsels! She was robbing me! But I had to have the food. I was salivating. I was probably drooling. I shook out another diamond. She took the jewels. I took the provisions.

It would have been decorous to take everything with me and eat in the privacy of zhamM's parlor. But I couldn't wait that long. While the gnomes watched with expressions of fascinated revulsion, I bit into the cheese.

It was hard and salty and full of flavor. I chewed it, sucked on it, almost swooned from pleasure. Then I gobbled up the grapes and the bun.

I hesitated over the apple, but it was human food, and I couldn't resist. I bit into it.

It wasn't bad, sweet and not mealy. I began to swallow, then tasted something under the sweetness, something bitter and searingly sharp. I tried to cough the morsel out, but it wedged in my windpipe. I clutched my throat to squeeze it out. It didn't budge. I tried again to cough. I tried to breathe. I staggered and fell.

The peddler bent over me, her expression a mix of remorse and gloating—just as zhamM had predicted.

Oh, Ijori! She'd poisoned me!

My essence was wrenched away from my body. I floated toward the cavern ceiling. I wanted to get back to my body, but my essence had no strength. I could feel my body. It seemed unmoving, but it was breathing, oh so shallowly, a wisp of air finding its way past the chunk of poisoned apple.

My essence reached the ceiling and passed into the rock itself. Rock felt no different from air. I emerged into open space and flew, gaining speed, above the ridge Uju and I had followed. I could still feel my body in Gnome Caverns, could still feel that thin dribble of breath go in and out.

High above the caverns, the trek that had taken days was accomplished in seconds. Mount Ormallo rose ahead, and there was Ontio Castle.

I was in the castle, hurtling over the Great Hall, through a corridor, through a door—Ivi's door—into Ivi's apartments, to the dressing table, into the hand mirror. Into the mirror!

CHAPTER THIRTY-THREE

I SCREAMED AND SCREAMED. I hid my head in my hands. I stopped screaming and moaned. I crouched and rocked.

A voice said, "Welcome—"

I drowned out the voice.

Oh, Ijori. Oh, zhamM.

Gradually, thoughts filtered in. Was I dead? How had I been transported here? Why?

I was still aware of my body in Gnome Caverns. It was as if a string, thin as an eyelash, connected me to that body. I sensed my body was cold, but it still breathed. I tried to get back to it. I couldn't.

I heard Skulni's voice over my moans.

"Look at me, Aza. There are things you must know before I may leave."

Ugh! That oily spider's voice.

"Everyone dies. You needn't go on about it so."

Did everyone go into a mirror after dying? Was this the afterlife?

But I wasn't dead if I could still feel my body breathe.

I continued to rock and moan. I don't know how long it was before I heard Skulni's voice again.

"You're fortunate to be here."

I raised my head. I was in a small beige chamber, just big enough for Skulni and me and the room's few furnishings: a dressing table, dressing table mirror, and a chair, where Skulni sat. The mirror was split, really only half mirror. The other half was a window, the two side by side.

Light and sound came in the window half. Through it I saw Ivi's ceiling with its fresco of a shepherd and his flock of sheep. I heard birds chirping in the distance and someone singing.

Oh, to be there! In the heaven of the world.

Skulni said, "I shan't be with you long."

I wouldn't be with *him* long. Thank heaven, there was a door. I went to it and grasped the knob, but I couldn't turn it, although I tried repeatedly.

I whimpered. Skulni laughed.

I grasped my overskirt. I was dressed in the gown I'd worn that last night in Ontio Castle. It was good as new, unsullied by prison or my brush with ogres. I pinched the cloth between my fingers and lifted it an inch. Easy as ever.

I tried again to turn the doorknob and failed again.

Why could I move one and not the other?

Because my gown wasn't real. My body—this one inside the mirror—wasn't real. I was an apparition. I looked down. The carpet pile stood straight up at the edge of my feet. I had no weight.

"Where am I?" My voice was hoarse.

"You know where you are. This is your last home."

A spider's web!

He had something of a spider's body: not much neck, a round belly in a tight-fitting blue doublet, round buttocks in blue hose, and spindly arms and legs, also garbed in blue.

I blurted out, "Are you human?"

He laughed again. "I should say not. I am the master of the mirror. There is none other like me."

Perhaps I had to destroy him in order to leave. I remembered the library keeper's words. *The mirror may be destroyed under certain unspecified circumstances.*

"But I appear human. Outside the mirror, I'm as large as anyone else, and I keep this face. *I* don't drink potions to make myself beautiful.

"Now you must learn about the mirror so I may leave. We have time before your queen returns from killing you."

I stared at him. "What had Queen Ivi to do with it?"

"She was the gnome who sold you the poisoned apple."

"But Ivi is human."

"The Disguises potion is very powerful. Under its influence, in many ways Ivi *was* a gnome."

I swayed and reached out to the wall to steady myself.

"Come, Aza. You know Her High High Highness's character." He said the words *High High Highness* with utter contempt.

Even Ivi couldn't be so bad!

"Comfort yourself with this: My powers will be yours when you sit in my chair. Come closer."

I hung back.

He drummed his fingers on the dressing table. They made no sound. He had no weight either.

"Don't you want to see?" He touched the mirror-window. "This is Ivi's hand mirror. You were curious enough about it when you were alive."

I was still alive. I approached the mirror and saw my former ugly face over his shoulder. "Did I change back?" I heard the alarm in my voice. I still cared.

He laughed. "Humans and beauty." My beautiful face returned. "That is your reflection." My original face replaced it. "That is my doing."

"Stop!"

He left my ugly face there. "When you sit in my seat, you dictate what appears. You can view moments in your life, your whole life if you like."

The scene changed. There was the Featherbed kitchen. It seemed small and cramped compared to the kitchen at Ontio Castle, but it looked cozy. Oh to be there! Ettime stood at the stove. Father came in from the tavern, carrying a tray of dirty glasses. His face was clean-shaven. It was his year without a mustache!

I saw myself, sitting on a stool, chopping celery, singing as I worked. I had never seen myself sing. I was concentrating on my song, and I looked happy. At that moment, at least, I wasn't thinking about being ugly.

"Enough!" Skulni said. "You can indulge yourself later. Observe how Her High High Highness came to own me."

Now I saw a richly furnished room, not so lavish as the queen's apartments, but lavish enough. A nightingale perched on the fireplace mantel. I heard a peep. The room had to be in Ontio Castle.

There was Ivi in her bridal finery, admiring herself in an oval mirror—Ivi, but a diminished version of the woman I knew, shorter and not so thin. Tiny frown lines were etched between her eyebrows, and her chin was weak. Her cheeks were marked by the scars of pimples, but her face was still appealing. Even then she was pretty.

A woman appeared behind her—appeared out of nothing.

"The fairy Lucinda," Skulni said, "who commands the mirror and thinks she commands me."

Lucinda was tall and stately, with long auburn hair, peacock-blue eyes, and generous full lips, far fairer than either Ivi or I in our beautified states.

Ivi saw the fairy reflected in the oval mirror. She turned and cowered.

Lucinda's lips moved, and miracle of miracles, I could hear her. "I am the fairy Lucinda. I adore weddings."

Ivi curtsied unsteadily.

"Darling," Lucinda said, "no need to be afraid. I'm here to give you a gift. This gift—"

"I wish you would make me as beautiful as you are." Ivi drew back, as if scared by her own audacity.

Lucinda smiled. "Darling, everyone is beautiful in her own way, and I am a fairy." She paused, then nodded. "I'll give you what you desire. My gift will make you as exquisite as you may be." She held out her hand, palm up. The magic mirror appeared atop her palm, and atop the mirror, the two vials of potion materialized. "Take it all."

Ivi accepted the gift in trembling hands.

"The potion bottles will refill themselves after they've been drained. You may make your betrothed as handsome as he can be, too, if you like, and anyone else, if your nature is generous."

I saw Ivi read the potion labels. She placed the mirror and the Disguises potion carefully on her washstand. Then she unstoppered the beauty-potion vial and drank.

The scene changed again.

Lucinda's face filled the mirror and beamed at Skulni and me. "Drinker of my potion," she said, "you have lived a happy life, beautiful into your old age."

"Fairy Lucinda," I said, my heart pounding, "I did not grow old."

Skulni said, "It's the fairy's speech to new arrivals. She can't hear you." He laughed. "She rarely listens even when she can. She spoke this to the first to die after owning me, the only one to live to a great age." He paused. "I was inexperienced then."

"Now you will enjoy the last benefit of the potions," Lucinda said. "Your existence will be extended in the mirror while Skulni has his much-deserved holiday. You shall remain here until I give the gift again. Then Skulni will return, and you will go to your final death. If you were generous with my gift, you will not be alone for long. The other potion drinkers will join you when they die."

Lucinda's face vanished, and the mirror's surface became blank. Skulni said, "The beautified reflection is my most useful power. It was my bait with you."

And I had taken it. "What did you want with me?"

x

"Surely you've worked that out by now. You're not a simpleton."

"What do you mean?"

Then I understood. The wicked, despicable bug! "You monster! You wanted me to drink the potion so Ivi would kill me and you'd have your holiday."

He smiled. "Just so. I was also trying to bring about Her High High Highness's death. The rebellion, you know. Whichever of you died first would do." He rose from his chair and went to the door. "And now I take my leave."

I watched him, paralyzed with horror. I should have taken his seat, but I didn't think of it.

He could no more turn the doorknob than I could. He faced me, his face red with rage. "You misbegotten lump, you hell cow, you miscreation . . ."

I fled to the opposite wall, as far from him as could be.

"You wouldn't drink all the potion, and now I'm imprisoned with you."

I hoped that wasn't why. I hoped it was because I was still alive.

The fury faded from his face. "It will be amusing when the queen dies and she joins you." He sighed. "Since you haven't released me, I'll have to cause her death." He sat again.

My mouth was dry. "How?"

"Oh, I have many methods. I've caused duels, wars, even famines."

"How will you make her do what you want?"

He smiled. "Exactly as I did before. Her Majesty is child's play. She craves admiration, which is easily given. She craves love even more, and that I can pretend to. These strategies are usually enough. But if she continues to resist my suggestions, I threaten to take away her beauty. That always succeeds with her."

CHAPTER THIRTY-FOUR

*T*HE ROOM SPUN. I sank to the floor.

Take away her beauty . . . I wondered what Skulni might have persuaded me into to preserve my own beauty.

Not murder. No, but how much better than Ivi was I, really?

Skulni said, "I didn't have to threaten anything to persuade her to kill you. Her own jealousy was quite enough. I only had to help her find the courage to do the deed."

"What will you have her do to cause her own death?"

"Hmm . . ." He leaned back and stared up at the ceiling.

I followed his eyes. The beige had darkened to gray, and the corners were obscured by shadow. Day was waning.

My body in Gnome Caverns was weakening. I felt my pulse slow.

He said dreamily, "I believe I'll get Her High High Highness executed."

I sat up straight. "How?"

"I'll persuade her to kill someone in the castle. Surely they'll execute her for that."

I could hardly make my mouth form the word. "Who?"

"I have three candidates in mind: your friend Uju, the king, and your prince."

I jumped up, vibrating with distress. "Not Ijori."

He began to laugh.

"Not any of them!" I pulled my paring knife from my reticule. I would stop him from doing more harm.

He laughed harder, and I knew I couldn't hurt him.

When he finished laughing, he said, "Of course, His Majesty might do my work for me when he recovers. He might execute her for killing you."

"But he won't know what she did."

"He may have heard every word his wife spoke at his bedside. It's happened before. I know of several cases." Skulni shrugged. "But I fear His Majesty's doting heart will stop him doling out the ultimate punishment. I shan't wait."

How could I dissuade Ivi from more murder attempts? She'd never listened to me in the past, but perhaps I could think of something to make her listen. "When will the queen return?"

He looked at me sharply. "Why do you wish to know?"

"I want to prepare myself for the sight of her."

"Ah. In two days, more or less. She has a horse. I'm hoping she meets up with an ogre."

If an ogre ate her, she'd arrive here, in the mirror, and everyone else would be out of danger.

I sought a way to foil Skulni if she came home safely. If only I could warn Ijori! I tried to will myself out of the mirror, to wherever he might be. If I was an apparition, why couldn't I float where I wanted? Feeling ridiculous, I jumped—and landed hard.

Skulni laughed at me.

Twilight was almost over.

"What happens at night?" I kept the tremble out of my voice, but I was frightened at the prospect of being alone in the dark with him.

"Nothing. We wait. Here, waiting is our lot."

A whimper escaped me.

A sob.

"Tears are tedious."

I wept. Apparition though I was, I could produce buckets of tears. Ijori would never again comfort me when I cried. I thought of Mother and Father and Areida and my brothers. I thought of all the songs I wouldn't write and wouldn't sing. I thought of zhamM. But mostly I thought of Ijori. Ijori. Dear heart. Sweet. Ijori. Dear heart. Sweet.

When I finally dried my eyes, I thought dawn would be

beginning. But our chamber was as dark as ever.

In the dark, where I couldn't see or be seen, I considered beauty and ugliness.

My ugliness had persuaded Sir Uellu I was part ogre. It had caused people—guests at the Featherbed, villagers in Amonta, courtiers and servants here in the castle—to be rude and cruel.

I'd had no chance to be beautiful in everyday circumstances, to be admired at the castle or at the Featherbed. Perhaps I would love the admiration, or perhaps it would bring less pleasure than I expected. Without doubt my beauty had prevented Uju from killing me, and I'd certainly enjoyed seeing myself beautiful in a mirror.

The *pursuit* of beauty, however, had been disastrous. The pursuit of beauty had turned me to stone. It had left me with a marble toe and had brought me here.

"You might sing to me," Skulni said. "It will pass the time."

I wouldn't.

"If you won't, I will." He sang in a whiny, singsong voice:

> *"I never sing myself to sleep,*
> *For plotting keeps me busy:*
> *Whom to kill and how to woo*
> *The foolish heart that owns me.*

"I'll stop if you'll sing."

I sang a riddle. Perhaps solving it would keep him quiet awhile. As soon as I began to sing, I felt better, stronger.

> "I sharpen ears
> And weaken eyes—
> Who am I?
>
> "Thieves love me
> Though I steal nothing—
> Who am I?
>
> "I linger long in winter,
> In summer I'm too soon gone—
> Who am I?
>
> "The silver queen rules me.
> I light her candles—
> Who am I?
>
> "Cereus is my flower,
> The owl is my bird—
> Who am I?"

Skulni said, "Easy. I might have needed a moment's thought if you'd sung during the day."

He'd gotten it. He was quick.

"Sing more," he said.

"I will if you'll give me a turn in your chair." I wanted to determine what Ivi saw from now on. Perhaps I could persuade her to shatter the mirror, although its destruction might be the end of me.

So be it. My body would stop breathing soon anyway.

"You may try the chair at dawn if you'll sing until then."

I began. He played on human failings. I sang every song I knew of human virtue. I sang of friendship, love, humor, kindness, self-sacrifice.

As I sang, I felt strong enough to fly. I wondered if my real body back in Gnome Caverns was mending. But no, I could feel it losing ground, the merest trace of air trickling down its windpipe.

Dawn came eventually.

I stopped singing. If I'd been in my real body, I'd have had a sore throat. "Stand up," I said. "Let me try the chair."

He laughed. "You believed me, and I had a night of beautiful music. Ivi believed—"

I rushed at him. I had to sit in his chair, or I couldn't talk to her. I tried to push him off. He tried to push me away. But we were empty clothing fighting, no muscle, no sinew.

CHAPTER THIRTY-FIVE

I RETREATED TO MY station by the curtains and battled with despair. Another day and a half until Ivi returned. It didn't matter when she came if I could do nothing.

Hours passed. Skulni sat, motionless, staring at the mirror. If I started him talking, I might learn something I could use.

"Have you been owned by Ayorthaians before?"

"Twenty-seven Ayorthaians, twenty-four of them female, none such an eyesore as you were."

Thank you. "Have you influenced Ayorthaian history?"

"I should say so. Your civil war over the king's council? I had a hand in that." He chuckled. "And before the civil war, your Queen Ursalu was one of my owners."

"She was assassinated!"

"Easily contrived." He laughed harder. "The fairy Lucinda has never once inquired into what I do. What a fool she is."

What a venomous spider he was.

He went on. He seemed to have been behind every trag-edy and catastrophe in our history.

When he was finally done, I asked, "What do you do when you're in the world?"

"Travel. I dislike being confined. I like to eat. I seek out new foods, excellent . . ."

He told me every kind of food he preferred. He named every inn that served a fine this or a fine that.

I gasped. "You were Master Ikulni! You came to the Featherbed!"

"The Featherbed? Hart with fire peppers? So tasty. I've never tasted—"

"Your money vanished after you left."

He laughed merrily. "The Featherbed!"

Night fell at last. We spent it in silence. I felt my body in Gnome Caverns fade by degrees.

Daylight returned. My third day in the mirror. Perhaps Ivi would arrive soon.

The breakfast hour came and went.

In Gnome Caverns I felt my heart falter and beat again, falter and beat.

Noon came and went.

I heard footsteps. Ivi's voice. "No. I need nothing, only solitude. I need to be alone."

A woman's voice. "Yes, Your Majesty."

I heard the door close. My heart here pounded in my ears. Ivi's face—her human face, not her gnome face—appeared in the mirror-window. A tear splattered on the glass. She was crying down on us.

"Oh, Skulni, come. Come."

"Your High High Highness, your lowly servant attends you."

"I killed her, didn't I? Did she really die?"

"You are the fairest once again."

I called out, "Ivi! I'm here."

She didn't hear me. "How could I have killed her? I used to like her so much. When she was the oaf, she was my friend."

The *oaf*!

She must have picked up the mirror. I felt no sense of movement, but my view of the ceiling around her face slid away, replaced by tapestry and wall. She continued to weep.

I yelled louder. "Ivi! Listen! Ivi!"

Again she didn't hear.

"My brave, brave queen, the oaf wouldn't have made herself beautiful if she had truly been your friend."

"But now she's dead. I'd have been content if she'd grown oafish again."

"Mourn her, my queen. I'd think less of you if you did not."

"I loved my poor oaf."

"Your loving heart is speaking. Your clever mind knows the beautiful Aza was your rival."

"That's true." She wiped her eyes. "She was my rival. She kissed Ijori."

"And he wished to marry her."

"She deserved to die."

"Your High High Highness, your lowly servant is worried for you."

She frowned. "Why? The oaf is dead, and you're watching out for me, and you'll always be faithful."

"And why will I always be faithful?"

She answered promptly. I could tell she'd said this many times. "Because you worship at my face."

Sickening!

"Yes," Skulni said, "I do. I'm worried because of the guard Uju. He is a danger to you."

Not Ijori! I felt a rush of joy and then shame. I didn't want Uju to die.

"How is he a danger?"

"You instructed him to kill your oaf."

"I didn't!"

"Not in so many words, but you promised to knight him if she died in his company. And you failed to knight him."

"He didn't kill her!"

"Yes, but he may be angry, perhaps angry enough to speak against you."

It was believable, maybe even true. I stood over Skulni, rising on my toes in frustration. Then I felt my heart in Gnome Caverns stop. A dozen seconds passed before it beat again.

On that beat I had an idea. I illused my voice over Skulni's mouth. "Your Majesty? It's Aza." Your oaf. I sang, "I'm in the magic mirror." As I sang, I felt my strength rise again.

Skulni waved his hand in front of his mouth, trying to erase my voice.

I illused and sang, "Skulni doesn't want you to know I'm here."

"Aza? Where are you?"

I sang, "In the mirror." As I sang, I looked down, trying to think of what to say. "Here, in the mirror." It was then that I noticed the carpet. While I sang, my feet sank into it. I had weight! I stopped singing. The carpet pile sprang back. Singing gave me true strength.

Ivi cried, "Are you still beautiful?"

"My queen," Skulni said, "don't—"

I slid my voice over his. "He's trying to get you killed. He lied to you. He—"

She screamed, "Are you still beautiful?"

I sang, no longer illusing, "Go away! Move! Go away!" I pushed Skulni off his chair. He was lighter than dust. I saw his startled face, creasing into fury.

I sat. The chair felt like an ordinary chair, but as soon as I was seated, I was linked to the mirror. It became as much a part of me as my hands, and using it was as easy as pointing. I thought what I wanted Ivi to see in the mirror. The image came to mind. I projected it.

First I showed her my former face.

She began to smile. "Aza!"

I showed her my present self and sang, "I'm still beautiful."

"Aza!" Her face dropped away, and her chamber swung by. I saw the ceiling again. Then I saw her hems and her slipper with its sharp heel coming our way.

Yes!

Was I about to die?

The slipper pounded on the mirror-window. It didn't break. Pounded again. Again. She was stamping on it.

But she couldn't smash it.

She tried other ways. She swung the mirror into her doorknob. She attacked it with her paring knife.

At my side, Skulni bowed and smiled a spider's smile.

I heard her shrieking, "I can't break you. Why can't I break you? Skulni, why can't I break you?"

I sang, "He wants to get you executed, so he—"

"Aza?" Her face was back. "After you died, you went into the mirror? With Skulni?"

I said yes.

"If I kill myself, will I be with you, too? Will I be?"

Skulni thrust his head next to mine and answered, "Yes, my queen. I've been longing for you."

"Then I'll do it. Skulni wants me, not you."

"No!" I cried.

She must have put us down. The mirror-window showed only the ceiling. Skulni crossed his arms, grinning mightily.

She was back. I saw her hands, pouring white powder into a tumbler.

"No!" I shouted. "Don't!" I tried to think of something to show her in the mirror. Then I thought what to attempt. I sang:

> *"I won't remain*
> *with Skulni,*
> *a monster, a spider*
> *in a mirror. . . ."*

Still singing, I leaped up, overturning the chair. My connection to it snapped. Still singing, I made a fist and punched the mirror with all my strength.

It sounded as if all the keys of a piano had been banged at once. A jagged crack formed, but the mirror held.

Ivi stirred the poison with a spoon. "Oaf, I'm coming. Ogress, I'm coming."

I sang, full voice, "Ijori! My love . . . Ayortha . . ." and struck the mirror again.

Another crack formed, but the mirror still held.

Ivi raised the tumbler.

I was a chorus, a choir. I threw myself—shoulders, elbows, knees, all my singing weight—into the mirror. I sang, "I won't remain in a mirror, a beauty in a—"

A roar drowned me out.

CHAPTER THIRTY-SIX

*T*HE MIRROR CRUMBLED in a bedlam of jangling notes.
Skulni shrieked as the walls crumbled, too. For a moment
he and I stood on Ivi's dressing table, each of us smaller than
a thimble. My feet were in a puddle, and I glimpsed shards
of the vials that had contained the potions. I saw Ivi drop
the tumbler.

I was lifted up and drawn backward toward the door.
As I went, I heard Ivi's cry of dismay and watched Skulni
dwindle and fade from sight. Then I was torn away, through
corridors and out of the castle. Again I whirred along the
Ormallo range. Again I was pulled through solid rock.

Below was the market cavern. I saw my body, covered by
a jeweled blanket, surrounded by pillows. zhamM knelt at
my side, holding my hand.

I swooped down. Oh! My face was no longer beautiful. I
slipped into myself.

The world disappeared. I couldn't move so much as a finger. I was a tiny flame, tinier than a candle's flame, buried deep in a glacier. I felt zhamM's hand and the weight of the blanket, but they were a mile away.

A wisp of air entered the glacier. My ribs rose the slightest bit. My heart beat weakly. Against the weight of a glacier it could do no more.

My heart beat again. And again. And stopped. My flame guttered. My heart beat. And stopped. And beat. I felt my consciousness fade. As my flame winked out, I heard a dog bark.

Someone raised me and struck my back. My mouth fell open. The apple flew out. I flared back to life. I breathed deeply, then fainted.

I awoke in my cavern bedchamber.

zhamM sat in a chair next to my bed. "Maid azacH?"

I smiled at him. I loved his kind, leathery face. I tried to thank him for saving me, but my mouth was too dry. I licked my lips.

"I have broth." He raised my back and piled pillows behind me. I was too weak to help. When I was propped up, he went to a brazier. He poured the broth and brought it to me in a steaming mug.

I held out my hands for the mug, but then I couldn't hold

it. zhamM hadn't let go, so nothing spilled.

My hands, on the mug, were wide with broad fingers. My old hands. Memories flooded in. Skulni. Ivi.

I tried again to speak.

"Wait. Let the broth cool. Drink and then tell me." He sat next to me on the bed, holding the mug.

I waited impatiently. Someone should go to Ontio Castle immediately, to protect Uju.

zhamM held the broth to my lips. I sipped. Root-vegetable broth. It tasted good anyway.

After a few swallows I found my voice. "widyeH zhamM, how long since I spat out the apple?"

"Only yesterday."

"How long since . . . since my appearance changed back?"

"Yesterday as well."

Then not so much time had gone by. That was a relief. I wondered if I'd really destroyed the mirror. If I had, what had happened to Skulni? Might he have been freed? Might he be in the castle now, as a man, working his wiles for his own ends?

"widyeH zhamM, Ivi gave me the poisoned apple." I tried to get out of bed, but I could hardly move the covers. "Guard Uju is in danger." Skulni hadn't had time to talk to Ivi about killing him, but he might have said enough to get Uju imprisoned or sent on a perilous mission.

"You need to rest," zhamM said. "widyeH bynoK, the physician, believes you'll be fine after food and a day's rest. Of course, to be exact, he's never treated a human before." He smiled. "But you're part gnome."

I smiled back. He was such a friend, to be exact. "Thank you. You saved me again."

"Not I. I only hovered and worried." His expression changed. "Your queen was here?"

"Disguised as a gnome."

"Maid azacH, a human couldn't disguise herself as a gnome. Not among gnomes."

"She drank a potion that changed her."

"Like your beauty potion?"

I nodded.

He said, "The prince should be told."

I'd never heard about any gnomish prince, only their queen. "What prince?"

zhamM hesitated. "Prince Ijori. We were going to wait un—"

My heart stopped again and then beat wildly. "Ijori!"

"Guard Uju told him where to find you. It was the prince who struck your back and forced out the apple."

"Where is he now?"

"He isn't part gnome. He can't live down here. He's camped outside our main gateway."

"Ogres!"

"Exactly outside, to be exact. If he sniffs even a whiff of a whiff of an ogre, he'll nip inside and shut the door." He stood. "I'll summon him."

"widyeH zhamM? Is my hair htun again?"

"Yes. It's beautiful."

"Would you bring back a mirror after you send for Ijori?"

He returned in a few minutes. I took the mirror, and my hand was strong enough to hold it.

I was myself once more. I had the face and shape I would keep always. I would have to learn to accept it. I wouldn't try again to transform myself.

Still looking in the mirror, I held my other hand out to zhamM. He took it. My hair *was* htun. Oh! It was beautiful.

Ijori and Oochoo came soon. Ijori rushed toward me but then stopped. Oochoo leaped on the bed and covered my face with kisses. Her tail wagged so wildly, the bed shook.

"Are you all right? Oochoo! Hop off!"

She continued to stand over me, panting and wagging.

I reached up and scratched her neck. "I'm fine."

Ijori sat on the edge of the bed and took my hand as cautiously as if it was made of glass.

zhamM, standing at the foot of the bed, said, "She's out of danger, Prince Ijori, although she's still weak." He added,

"Are you hungry, Maid azacH?"

I nodded.

"I'll fetch food. After we eat, we can talk." Most considerate of gnomes, he left the cavern.

Ijori embraced me gently. Into my hair he murmured, "You look yourself again. I'm glad." He kissed my forehead, my nose, and my lips. "I thought you had died." He stroked my cheek. "While I was searching for you, word came from the castle that you'd died."

"We sent someone to tell you the truth."

"I blamed myself. If I had believed you, if I had argued for you, they might not have imprisoned you, and you wouldn't have run away."

He smelled of the sun.

"I went to Uju to hear about your death. He saw my grief and told me the truth. Then, when Oochoo and I arrived, I again thought you dead."

I kissed him. Oochoo barked and wagged. Ijori held me and hummed the melody I'd sung when we first kissed. My cheek learned the contour of his shoulder. Twice I opened my mouth to tell him about Ivi and Uju. Twice I closed it. These moments were too sweet to break into. Oochoo curled up next to us. I wanted to stay as we were forever.

zhamM returned with food. We broke away. Ijori fetched a chair and placed it by my bedside, next to zhamM's chair.

I said, "Ijori, the queen—"

"First you must eat." zhamM put a tray across my lap. "Prince Ijori, I brought a plate of parsnips and potatoes for you, too, and for me, Maid azacH's favorite, tree roots."

I laughed and grimaced, then tucked into my vegetables. After a bite or two, I thought to say, "Thank you for saving me, Ijori."

"It was Oochoo," he said. "widyeH zhamM and I thought you dead, but Oochoo barked."

I didn't understand.

He explained. "She's been in skirmishes with ogres. She whimpers over the dead, but she barks over the wounded."

I stroked her ears. She put her head on my thigh and looked longingly at my plate. Ijori reached into the pocket of his tunic and slipped her a treat.

At the end of the meal, zhamM said, "Prince Ijori, Maid azacH said dire doings may be taking place at your castle. How do you know this, Maid azacH?"

I explained how Ivi had been disguised as a gnome.

Then I told them about being transported into the mirror, about Skulni, about Ivi's return and the mirror's destruction. At the end I said, "I fear for Uju."

Ijori said, "I'll return to Ontio in the morning. widyeH zhamM, Aza will be safe here now, won't she?"

zhamM said, "Quite—"

I sang, "I'm coming too. I may be needed." I knew Ivi better than anyone.

zhamM sang in a rumbling bass, "Maid azacH, don't go."

Ijori sang, "It's too dangerous. They'll imprison you again, and the queen wants to kill you."

I sang, "If you don't let me come, I'll run away and follow on foot."

They argued with me, presenting many reasonable reasons.

"The king is better," I said. "Soon he'll be able to judge me. I'll be content to put myself in his hands. If the king's council wants me to go back to prison until then, I'll go, and I won't escape."

They gave up, and Ijori left us. He had begun to shift in his chair, because the caverns were troubling him.

In the morning the gnomish physician declared me strong enough to travel. I still felt weak, but I kept that to myself.

zhamM accompanied me to the cavern gateway, where Ijori and Oochoo were waiting with six gnomes and nine horses. I blinked in the sunlight. I hadn't been outside—except as an apparition—in seven weeks. zhamM said he and the others would ride with us for the first day.

"After that I think you'll be safe from ogres."

We mounted the horses and set out. Oochoo stayed close.

Ijori said she would, so long as she smelled ogres. The gnomes became noisy and merry, joking in Gnomic and guffawing. zhamM had never been so boisterous in my presence. Ijori and I exchanged worried glances. Any ogres within five miles would hear us.

zhamM saw our faces. In a low voice while the others continued their banter, he said, "Maid azacH, Prince Ijori, this is how we behave when ogres are about. We want them to hear us. Adult gnomes are too leathery for them. They break their teeth on us. If they hear us, they stay away."

I whispered, "If they won't eat you, why do you care if they find you?"

"They're still persuasive and still dangerous." He cocked his head at his companions and smiled. "I assure you, we do not enjoy having so much fun."

It's not easy to tell that humor in a foreign tongue is forced, but now I noticed the gnomes were frowning as they laughed. Two were concentrating so hard, they were squinting.

It was a hot summer day. The sun was pitiless. Nonetheless, it was splendid to be outside. I'd thought I'd never again see anything as big as the sky, or travel through a landscape, or take in deep swallows of the world's air.

We saw no sign of ogres. By afternoon I was weary, but I forced myself to sit straight and endure. I recalled songs and tried not to think, although some thoughts came. If all went as well as we could hope—Uju unharmed, the king's council persuaded that I'd committed no crime—Ivi would still be queen. I didn't know if I'd be safe at the castle, or anywhere in Ayortha.

When we forded a stream at dusk, zhamM declared that we had crossed to greater safety. We camped together, and the gnomes took their leave in the morning. I sang—softly—a farewell song to zhamM. I had stayed awake late composing it in my mind.

> "I can never stop thanking you.
> If I never stop,
> I never need to say
> farewell.
> A river rushes between us.
> You follow it north,
> I pursue it south.
> When I weep
> because I miss you,
> my tears will seep
> through your cavern.
> Your face is kind
> as a shawl in winter,
> or a diamond for a song.

My family keeps an inn.
You have a chamber in my heart.
No rent is due.
Farewell.
Farewell."

CHAPTER THIRTY-SEVEN

*I*t took Ijori and me another day and a half to reach the castle. The danger of ogres must not have been significant, because Oochoo began to leave us for her own explorations. Still we were prudently quiet. But dozens of times our eyes met and we smiled.

We spent the night in a ravine, perhaps the same one Uju and I had sojourned in, lying on hard sandy ground under an overhanging rock. We had whispered for a while, planning. First, we would warn Uju. Ijori would try to keep Ivi away from me. When the king was well enough, I would tell him my story and let him judge me.

We fell silent. I stared at the quarter moon while Oochoo snuggled her head against my shoulder.

"Ijori? The queen may not be so beautiful now."

"Mmm . . . what?" He must have been halfway to sleep.

"She drank the potion earlier than I did, before her wedding."

"If she looks as she behaves, she'll have the face of a viper."

"People don't—" I stopped. I was almost shouting.

Oochoo rose over us, her tail down and wagging.

I whispered, "People don't look as they behave."

Oochoo settled against Ijori.

"Oh, love, I never . . ." He paused. "Sweet, I adore your face and your hands and the scent of your skin and the thicket of your hair. When I saw you on the receiving line, I thought you had grandeur."

"I was frozen with fright and blushing scarlet!"

"Nonetheless, that's what I thought. You have grandeur and dignity. I was sorry when you became beautiful in a commonplace way."

Oh. Oh, my.

I had grandeur. I breathed in the cool night air. Perhaps I could learn to wear myself without apologies, with dignity. Perhaps I could become what Ijori already saw. Perhaps someday I might even be able to smile at myself in a mirror.

Not yet. But maybe someday.

I reached out and touched his cheek. He caught my hand and held it. Oochoo rolled over on her back, legs in the air.

"Ijori?"

He was asleep. I didn't wake him. We spent the night clasping hands.

We crossed the castle drawbridge early the next afternoon. A groom took our horses.

Ijori asked, "How fares the king?"

The groom answered distractedly, staring at me, "He is no better. The physician says he is losing ground."

Ijori fell back a step. I took his hand, not caring if the groom saw.

"The physician believes he is pining for the queen."

"Where is she?" I said.

"She's here. First she sneaked out of the castle and stayed away for several weeks. Now she's shut herself in her chambers. She refuses to let anyone in, and she won't come out. She won't visit her husband."

The potion had lost its effect on her, too, and she didn't want people to see her. I wondered if she knew the king was worsening.

The groom began to walk our horses away, but Ijori stopped him. "Do you know anything of a guard named Uju?"

The man mumbled something.

"Speak up!" Ijori said.

"Begging your pardon, Your Highness, but Uju said

she"—he cocked his head at me—"was dead. He must have been mistaken."

Ah, good. If Uju had been in prison, the groom would have told us that first. We turned toward the castle courtyard. I heard a troubadour and birdsong, just as I had on my first arrival.

I swallowed. "I'll go to the queen." I was the only one who might convince her to visit the king. I didn't want an encounter with her. The thought of it made me feel the poison in my throat again. But if King Oscaro's recovery hung in the balance, I had to do what I could.

When we stepped into the Great Hall, silence spread from us in a widening ripple. I think even the songbirds quieted. We ignored everyone and hurried to Ivi's room. I knocked on her door.

"Go away. Leave me."

I turned the knob. The door was locked.

"It's Aza," I called. I knew what I had to say to have a chance at admittance, but I hated saying it. "I'm no longer beautiful, Your Majesty."

A moment passed, and then the lock turned.

"Only you."

Ijori whispered, "Shout if you need me. I'll break down the door."

She allowed barely enough space for me to squeeze in. As

soon as I entered, she locked the door behind me.

The curtains were drawn. The room was in shadow. I only glimpsed Ivi's face, not enough to tell anything.

I looked at her vanity table. No hand mirror. No golden flute.

She flung herself on her bed, facedown. Her voice was muffled. "I thought you were somewhere with Skulni. Where is he?"

"The mirror's magic ended. He's gone." I hoped this was true. I hoped I hadn't freed him.

"I miss him." Her voice rose. She pounded the mattress with her fist. "I want him."

I conjured him up in my mind. He knew how to manage her. I heard his spider voice, and it spoke the words I needed.

"Skulni adored you," I said. "Before you came back from Gnome Caverns, he told me how much he cared for you."

She rolled over. "He did?"

I saw her face. She no longer resembled a tragic heroine when she cried. She looked as the rest of us do—her skin was blotchy and her nose was red.

I continued. "He said you were his favorite, of all his years in the mirror. He called you *gallant*." Perhaps I was overdoing it.

She sat up. "Aza! He said that?"

Now to help the king: "Skulni loved you almost as much as His Majesty does."

She threw herself back down, face in the counterpane again. "Nobody loves me."

"The king does! He leaped in front of the centaur's iron ring for you. Your life is more precious to him than his own. Even—"

"Not anymore. Not now that I'm—"

"You're still beautiful," I said, gritting my teeth. "And you know how to keep a beau. You told me so. You said no minxes ever took one from you."

"Oh, Aza . . ." She sat cross-legged on the bed. "I'm so glad you didn't—" She stopped herself.

Didn't die?

She smiled at me. "We can be friends again. I know more ways to fix your hair."

My htun hair was fine as it was. But I made myself smile back. "Would you like to go to the king? He is longing for you."

She wanted to, but first she had to choose the most becoming gown, and I had to tell her she was ravishing in every one she tried. Then came the hair, which was wispy and fine now. She pinned it up and let it down at least a dozen times. Last came the cosmetics, another anxious business.

Finally she was finished, and I had to admit she showed

herself to her best advantage. She was lovely.

I still felt a pang that others could be lovely and not I.

When we stepped into the corridor, Ijori's face registered no surprise at the change in her. "Your Majesty." He bowed and then held out his arm.

She took it. I positioned myself on her other side. We set off for the physician's chambers. Songbirds serenaded us as we went. We passed servants and courtiers, who stared and then bowed or curtsied. Ivi nodded and ignored the stares.

She stopped a yard from the king's sickroom and touched her hair. She straightened her gown. Then she turned to me and whispered, "He loves me? He still loves me?"

It was far better to be me than to be Ivi. "He loves you."

"No minx will take him from me now either." She opened the door.

King Oscaro sat in a chair facing the window. His expression when he turned to us was melancholy, but it changed to joy when he saw Ivi. He couldn't speak, but his smile was eloquent enough. If he noticed any alteration in her, his face didn't show it.

She ran to him. "My Lord." She knelt, gazing up at him.

He drew her to him in an awkward embrace.

Ijori tugged on my arm. We backed out of the room and closed the door behind us.

CHAPTER THIRTY-EIGHT

WHEN WE LEFT the king, we found Uju and warned him to take care. However, now that Ivi had been reunited with her husband, I thought Uju in little danger.

The king's council members spent the entire next day deliberating and came to the conclusion—despite Ijori's explanations and arguments—that they didn't know what to make of me. Furthermore, they feared I might still be dangerous. Their reasons: I could illuse; my appearance had changed twice; and I had magically escaped from prison. The council decided to confine me to my bedchamber with two guards at my door. When—and if—the king was well enough, he would judge my case.

Visitors were allowed. Ijori spent much of each day with me, and he wasn't my only companion. Uju came too. So did Mistress Audra and the tailor. We sang together, and the guards often opened the door, the better to hear us and to sing along. Then, naturally, passersby stopped to listen too, and to join in, and to enter and sing more.

Castle opinion mounted in my favor. I was no longer constantly at Ivi's side—indeed, she never visited me. Mistress Audra and the tailor were my enthusiastic advocates, and even taciturn Uju spoke up for me.

One afternoon Mistress Audra asked me to show everyone how to illuse. No one could do it, but it became the fashion to stop by for a demonstration. My prison was frequently the merriest spot in the castle.

Sometimes I asked my visitors if they'd seen anyone resembling Skulni. The answer was always no. I prayed he'd truly been destroyed, destroyed beyond return in some other form.

After he saw Ivi, King Oscaro's recovery resumed. A week later he spoke to her, his first halting words. "My . . . dear . . . beautiful . . . love."

Exactly what she'd want to hear.

I was overjoyed he was better, but I was dismayed, too. Soon I'd be brought before him, and I'd tell him terrible truths about Ivi. Would he believe them? Or would he deem me an ill-favored, lying ogre's cousin?

The following Tuesday I was summoned to the Throne Room. Ivi was at the market in Ontio with her new lady-in-waiting, the plain-faced daughter of a knight.

I was as frightened as I'd been during my first time in the king's presence.

He spoke slowly, and he formed his words deliberately, but each one was clear, and his sentences were complete and lucid. "Thank you . . . for . . . coming . . . , Maid Aza. I am . . . hoping . . . you can . . . explain . . . some matters . . . I don't . . . understand."

Then he asked Sir Uellu to remain in the chamber with us, but no one else.

I told them almost everything, from the moment Ivi found me illusing to my assurance to her of the king's love. I omitted only her habit of flirting with Ijori and Uju. I couldn't omit her attempt on my life, but I stressed Skulni's evil influence. I wanted to ameliorate the king's pain. Moreover, I wanted to present myself as fair.

They let me speak without interruption, but I interrupted my story once. I couldn't help myself. When I first mentioned the potions, I said, "Sire, did you notice a change in Her Majesty's appearance at the wedding, and again recently?"

He nodded. His expression didn't change. I waited for him to say something, but he was silent. I resumed my tale.

Sir Uellu shook his head occasionally, but King Oscaro looked steadily at me, his expression unfailingly attentive.

At the end he turned to the choirmaster. With an effort

he said, "I . . . believe her. I wish the truth were otherwise, but I believe it. Queen Ivi told me some of it herself."

As Skulni had suggested, the king had heard what she'd told him when he'd been in his apparent stupor.

The king added, "I didn't comprehend everything. I was most perplexed by the mirror she spoke of."

Sir Uellu said, "Sire, how appalling. Maid Aza—" He sang,

> "I'd give my best notes
>   for forgiveness.
> I was wrong,
>   my ears confused.
> I cannot undo the deeds
>   or erase the need
>   for forgiveness."

I said nothing. I wasn't ready to forgive him.

He went on, "What will you do to the queen, Your Majesty?"

"I shall do nothing *to* her. She saved my life, and I love her. When I lay on my sickbed, I was a wanderer in a shadowy wilderness. If not for her I would still be wandering. When she came to me at night, her voice was my guide. Her presence was my solace. In my delirium I thought her a cat.

She was a small black cat, and she led me home.

"I shall do nothing to her, but I must do something so that she may never again rule Ayortha."

He asked us to leave.

Ijori was waiting anxiously outside. As soon as he saw my expression, he knew all was well. He kissed me right before Sir Uellu. But a kiss wasn't enough to express his joy. He spun me around and fed Oochoo a handful of treats.

Sir Uellu apologized to me again and added, "I should have known by your marvelous voice that you couldn't be evil."

I shook my head. "Voices and faces aren't manifestations of good or bad." I realized how much I'd changed since I'd first arrived at the castle. I'd corrected the choirmaster!

He bowed and left us.

Ijori took my hands in both of his. "Aza?" He sang, "Aza? Oochoo? Aza?"

I waited, puzzled.

He laughed. "I've been to Kyrria and to Pu. I've addressed the twin kings of Bizidel and offended neither one, but I've never . . . Aza, I need a partner in the composing game . . ."

I smiled. "Of course."

He put a finger on my lips. ". . . a partner who raises me above myself . . ."

He wanted a different partner, not me?

". . . a partner who delights her listeners. Aza, will you marry me?"

I put my hand in front of my face. Then I lowered it, in spite of my blush. I sang, "I would marry you this moment. I'll harmonize with you forever."

We kissed again and again. Oochoo barked. I dared to reach into Ijori's tunic jacket for a treat for her.

The king spent the next morning alone with Ijori. Afterward he called for a Sing for the following week. It would be his first since he'd been injured. It would be my first since before being imprisoned.

Over the course of the week I wrote my song, taking extra care, eager to strike the right note. When the song was written, I went through my new gowns and chose a dusty pink one with a low loose waist and a pale-pink V-shaped collar. I was brave and looked at myself in the mirror.

Ugly.

Can a dragon judge ostumo?

I blinked in astonishment, realizing for the first time that I was as hard on myself as my worst critics. Sir Uellu had called me an ogre's cousin, and I'd believed he might be right. I'd thought Ijori saw me as hulking and unwomanly. I'd anticipated insults before they came. I'd avoided looking in actual mirrors, but I'd gazed constantly in the mirror in my mind and always hated what I showed myself.

I looked again in the real mirror in front of me.

Dignified. Dignified and grand.

I closed my eyes and saw myself again. Milk-white face, blood-red lips. Dignified and grand.

I reviewed my song and changed a word or two.

At the Sing I sat next to Ijori, with Oochoo sitting at attention between us. King Oscaro and Ivi entered. The king seated himself next to me and placed Ivi on his other side. I tightened my grip on Ijori's hand.

The Sing began. Everyone was in fine voice. The choral selections were sung with such fervor, Sir Uellu's baton could hardly keep up. Then, in a break from tradition, King Oscaro sang his solo first. He mounted the stage, his step as firm as it had ever been. He nodded at the choirmaster and began an epistolary song, the form Ivi had used at the Healing Sing.

> *"My dear friends, dear to me every one,*
> *"It is a joy to sing with you again. I can*
> *hardly believe I can. It is a joy to see your joy."*

People clasped hands and swayed and closed their eyes.

"I heard your voices when I was ill. I was adrift. I could find no path. My spirit was missing. I heard one voice above the rest. It found me. It told me stories I could not understand. At night it rested at my side. I thought it was a cat. I followed it home, where it turned into my love. My queen cured me, and I'll thank her forever."

People stopped swaying and opened their eyes. He held out his hand, and Ivi joined him on the stage, smiling triumphantly.

"She will leave me soon, for a brief while. She will live at Adoma, where the obirko blooms best."

The swaying resumed. Adoma was the king's southernmost castle.

"I've been your king for seventeen years, seventeen years of happiness, since a month before my nephew was born. I will be your king for three years more."

I heard huffs of surprise and a moan or two.

> *"When my reign is twenty years old and my nephew is, too, I will abdicate, and he will rule. His voice will carry, and Ayortha will be safe. Oochoo's voice carries farther, so Ayortha will be safer."*

There was laughter.

> *"And I daresay his wife's voice will carry farthest, so Ayortha will be safest."*

I listened and heard no gasps, felt no resentment. Thank you, everyone. Ijori squeezed my hand.

> *"We will have a new Three Tree on the throne—king, queen, and dog—bass, alto, and howl."*

More laughter.

> *"But although I step down, we will visit. I will sing with you through low times and high.*
>> *"Yours in loving gratitude,*
>>> *"Oscaro"*

The king was sending Ivi into exile so the rest of us would be safe from her. He had been both just and merciful. He was exiling himself as well. How much that pained him I have no idea.

He stepped back. I felt everyone stiffen as Ivi began to sing.

> "*Dear Subjects,*
>
> "*I am glad my husband is well again. I have not yet stopped smiling for joy. I hope you may tell by my violet gown, violet for happiness. It was a privilege to rule you for the months of my rule. I meant to be a strong queen. I thought you'd want a strong queen. I regret taking away your songbirds. I'm sorry. I didn't know how much you like them.*
>
> > "*Your king's happy wife,*
> > "*Queen Ivi*"

Her voice was weak, and she missed some notes, but her tune was pleasant. Every hand went up, and her smile grew and glowed.

She left the stage, but the king remained. I wondered why.

The doors at the back of the hall opened—and Mother and Father entered. I jumped up. Behind them were Ollo and

Yarry and Areida. And there was the duchess, and Dame Ethele! Ijori's smile was wide enough to touch his ears.

I ran up the aisle—and saw zhamM in the doorway. zhamM!

Oochoo pelted by and jumped up on Father. Mother embraced me, and I reached out for zhamM. Areida patted my back, and Yarry said, "Congratulations, Sister. I suppose the guards won't be back to arrest us all."

We laughed, and even the duchess looked glad.

zhamM said, "Congratulations, Cousin. You are at another crossroads, a splendid one, to be exact."

I didn't know I was at a crossroads.

Ijori took my hand. "Come, Aza." He sang softly in my ear, "We planned it in secret to confound the fairy Lucinda. We need no magical gifts." He reddened. "And I wanted to see your joy when your family came. It's our wedding day, love."

Sir Uellu sang, "Prince Ijori!"

"Yes, Ayortha!" Ijori tugged me down the aisle, just as Lady Arona had all those months ago for the composing game.

Sir Uellu sang, "Maid Aza!"

My knees were weak, my heart was hammering, but I was very, very happy. I mustered my voice and sang, "Yes, Ayortha!"

Hands went up.

Sir Uellu sang, "Ayorthaiana!"

Everyone sang, "Yes, Ayortha!"

Sir Uellu led us in the Three Tree Song.

Ijori sang next, a promise to Ayortha and a love song.

> *"Everything comes in threes.*
> *My love returned.*
> *Our king has sung.*
> *Tonight we wed.*
> *Everything comes in threes:*
> *My bride's voice,*
> *Our song together,*
> *Ayortha's chorus.*
> *Everything comes in threes.*
> *The king will uncurl his roots*
> *From his umbru throne.*
> *I'll be planted in his place.*
> *Aza will rise at my side.*
> *Everything comes in threes.*
> *Obirko, almyna, umbru.*
> *Council, king, kingdom.*
> *King, queen, Ayortha.*
> *I won't rule alone."*

I decided against the song I'd planned. "This is an Amontan love song," I began.

> "Every curl is a reason I love you
>   your fingers make ten more
>   each smile, each glance, each word
>   the reasons reach heaven"

People swayed and closed their eyes. Many clasped hands. I sang with my whole voice.

> "loving you makes me love myself more
>   loving you makes me love you evermore"

I added the final stanza of the song I'd written for the Sing.

> "I'm an innkeeper's daughter."

I saw Father beam.

> "A castle is an inn,
>   and a kingdom is a castle.
>   The regions are the rooms.
>   I know how to keep an inn.
>   An innkeeper does her best."

I began to illuse. From above the duchess's seat I sang in her voice, "My ostumo is piping hot." From above Uju's seat I sang in his voice, "My centaur is well stabled." From above the library keeper's seat I sang in his voice, "My books have fine titles, not overused." From above zhamM's seat I sang in his voice, "My bed is wide, to be exact." From above Frying Pan's seat I illused bells jingling. I sang in her voice, "The kitchen is ringing." I heard her shout of laughter. From my own mouth I sang, "I rejoice the king is well."

We left the stage and descended into a forest of waving arms.

EPILOGUE

S KULNI HAS NEVER been seen or heard from again in Ayortha.

Ivi didn't come to Ijori's coronation. Instead, she visited her home in the Kyrrian town of Bast, where she distributed gifts and harvested adulation. In the years that followed, she rarely came to Ontio, but her husband visited often and was always glad to share his wisdom with us.

I began to accompany Ijori on raids against the ogres. In time they discovered the trick of illusing, but they couldn't stop being fooled by it. Thus we made our roads and even the mountains safer for our subjects who traveled—a boon to the kingdom's innkeepers.

The Featherbed became the most popular and prosperous inn in Ayortha. As they grew older, Mother and Father left most of the labor to Yarry and Ollo and spent more and more time at court. Areida lived at court after she completed finishing school. She apprenticed herself to Sir Enole and became a fine physician. And she was always a close friend of the Kyrrian ruler, Ella of Frell.

The duchess and Dame Ethele took up residence at court too. Dame Ethele's gowns drove the tailor to such distraction that he designed a new wardrobe for her, colorful and intricate, but tasteful.

Because of the duchess, the castle's cat population swelled and the rat population dwindled. A kitten adopted Oochoo and followed her everywhere. Oochoo lived to a great age and was the best friend of each of our three children. She bayed when they sang, howled when they cried, and frolicked when they laughed.

I didn't try to change my appearance again. But fashions in beauty change, and perhaps my ascension to royalty hastened the alteration. Pulpy cheeks never became the rage, but my complexion came to be called vivid. My size became stately. Only Ijori deemed me a beauty, but I was considered handsome.

The children resembled him, although each of them had htun hair. Furthermore, they could see htun when zhamM held their hands.

I never discovered the identities of my birth parents. But zhamM consulted his family tree and found a great-great-great-grandmother who had married an Ayorthaian count.

It was possible that we truly were cousins. Our children were his cousins, too, and they could illuse as well as sing.

And so, with song and love, Ijori and I, our family, and our beloved kingdom lived happily ever after.

Fairest

An Interview with Gail Carson Levine

When Ivi Was Wren: A Deleted Chapter of *Fairest*

**A Sneak Peek at Gail Carson Levine's Next Novel,
*A Tale of Two Castles***

An Interview with Gail Carson Levine

Do you always write in the same place?
I write anywhere: airports, planes, trains, cars (when I'm not driving!), and at home. When I was learning to write, I read *Becoming a Writer* by Dorothea Brande. In that book there's an exercise that trains the aspiring author to write anywhere at any time.

What's your workspace like?
When I'm home, I do most of my writing in my office, which is in our very old house. The ceiling is low and the two windows are small—as they were in houses built before central heating—so it's quite cozy. I have file drawers, a desk, a computer, a printer, and bookshelves. Some of the books are for reference, including four books on English usage, how-to books on writing, several fairy-tale books, and books on fashion history. The walls are painted a soft blue. Hanging on them are two children's book illustrations by Cor Hazelaar, a childhood drawing of me by my sister, and five framed photographs taken by my husband—including a shot of our dog, Baxter, sleeping. One window faces the road, but the other looks out on our backyard: flowers spring and summer, a huge hemlock, bushes, several ancient maples, and the old outhouse (no longer in use). I adore my office.

When you are not writing children's books, what do you write?
I write poems for adults about whatever is going on in my life. Some of my poems are sad.

How much research do you do for your books in general? What did you read or learn for Fairest in particular?

The amount of research depends on the book. I certainly did the most for *Dave at Night*, because it's historical fiction, and I wanted to be as accurate as I could. For *Fairest*, which is fantasy, I mostly looked at books on fashion history, both to get the terms right and to see what people wore. I jumped from century to century, so there is no historical consistency. Almost all of Ivi's and Dame Ethele's costumes came from real outfits. The things that men and women wore were astonishing and often hideous. And I haven't even mentioned the hats!

How many times do you revise a book before it is published?

I revise as I write. By the time I finish a first draft I may have saved fifty versions in my computer. Once I have a first draft that I think is more or less reasonable, I may revise it three or four times before I send it to my editor. Then I may revise twice for her before the manuscript goes to the copy editor. After the copy editor sends me her edits, I usually see the book three or four more times, and each time I make changes. Then, *whew!* it's published. If I happen to look at it afterward, I always find things I wish I could change.

Do you write from a strict outline?

I don't outline at all, strict or otherwise. But when my story is based on a traditional fairy tale, the fairy tale itself gives me something to follow.

In Fairest, Aza and Ivi both get into trouble because they want to be more beautiful. What is your own relationship to beauty, and how has it changed over the course of your life?

I was a hippie in the '60s and '70s, and hippies weren't allowed to be very beauty-conscious. There was a code. Eyeliner was allowed, the thicker the better, but lipstick was a violation. Still, I wanted to look good. I am not exempt from caring about beauty. My first college boyfriend criticized me because I dressed too well! Now, many years later, I dislike the changes that aging brings, both external and internal: the wrinkles, the aching knee, the effects of gravity and time. In my books I usually write about what interests and worries me, and beauty does both. We want to present ourselves as attractively as we can, which is reasonable. Still, a glance at the cover of almost every magazine reveals that we care too much. Much too much.

When Ivi Was Wren:
A Deleted Chapter of *Fairest*

This is taken from a much earlier draft of Fairest. Ivi's name at that point was Wren, and the King's name was Otto. Wren's brother, Milo, and her mother, Effie, are characters, although they don't appear in the published book, and Lucinda is here in all her craziness. This draft is in the first person told from zhamM's point of view.

A stranger stood in the room with them. She hadn't come through the door, and she hadn't flown in the window. She was beautiful, so beautiful that Wren's comeliness seemed unexceptional and uninteresting. The stranger was tall and stately, with long auburn hair, peacock-blue eyes, and generous full lips.

She beamed at the humans and enjoyed their astonishment—all three of them frozen with their mouths forming perfect Os. "I am the fairy Lucinda. I adore weddings and brides and bridegrooms." She held her arms out to Wren and Milo.

Wren curtsied, looking pale and frightened.

Milo bowed. "I'm only the bride's brother." He wondered why she'd revealed herself. Fairies almost never did.

Lucinda shifted her full attention to Wren. "Darling, you needn't be afraid. I'm here to give you a gift."

Effie curtsied. "I'm Mistress Effie, the mother of the bride."

Lucinda continued. "This gift—"

"I wish you could make me as beautiful as you are." Wren drew back, scared by her own audacity.

"I thought you wanted steadfastness," Milo said.

Lucinda frowned at Wren's interruption and then smiled at her compliment. "Darling, everyone is beautiful in her own way,

5

and I am a fairy." She thought for a moment. She had planned to give the bride and groom one of her favorite wedding presents, the gift of always being together. But she could give them something else. She nodded, deciding. "I'll give you what you desire. My gift will make you as exquisite as a mortal may be." She held out her hand, palm up. A large box appeared on it, wrapped in gold-leaf paper and tied with a purple satin bow. She set the box down on the bed. "Go on, darling, open it."

Wren's hands trembled.

"Don't tear the paper, dear," Effie said.

Wren and Effie removed the paper gingerly to reveal a pasteboard box. Wren opened the box. Within was another box—an intricately carved wooden one—and a mirror. The mirror wasn't much larger than her face. It was framed in silver with a silver handle.

Wren looked at herself in the mirror. For a moment she saw her reflection, but then the glass turned cloudy. She caught her breath. Effie leaned close to see why.

Milo stood apart, feeling vaguely troubled. He thought Wren would benefit from less beauty, not more.

A man's face appeared in the mirror. It was neither old nor young, with a narrow nose, small pursed lips, and sharp eyes that took in the three humans at once.

The face in the mirror spoke. "The maiden is passable, but hundreds are prettier. Her mother was lovely a dozen years ago, but time has not been kind. The brother's nose is impossible, as large as a cucumber."

Milo, who liked his nose, was pleased with the comparison, but his unease increased.

The mirror continued. "The fairy is a delight to behold." Its eyes snapped back to Wren. "I suggest you make use of the wooden box immediately. I dislike the sight of you."

Lucinda's laugh was musical, burbling. "Dennis never minces words. Now open your box, darling."

Wren put the mirror back on the bed and picked up the box. For a moment she had trouble with the clasp. Then she got it and the box sprang open. Inside was a garden-variety cosmetics set and a tortoiseshell comb. She was disappointed, but knew better than to say so to a fairy. "Thank you, but I've already combed my hair, and Mother doesn't let me paint my face."

"Try the comb, darling, and your mother may make an exception about the rest, just this once."

Wren took off her snood and shook out her hair. Holding the mirror in one hand, she ran the comb through the hair on the left side of her face. The hair going into the comb was light brown, fine, and wispy. The hair coming out was a golden honey color, thick, and nine inches longer than it had been, long enough to reach the small of her back.

Effie said, "Oh!"

Milo gasped.

Wren dropped the comb and fainted.

Milo went to her, but before he reached her, she awoke. Frantically, she felt the floor for the comb. She shoved her skirts aside and found it. Without bothering to stand, she combed the rest of her hair as quickly as she could.

"I can feel it growing!"

"Of course you can, darling."

From the bed, Dennis (the mirror) said, "Worse than before. Your hair and face don't match. Quick. The cosmetics."

Effie said, "Go ahead, dear. Hurry."

Wren picked up the powder puff.

Milo snatched it away from her. He said wildly, "Don't.

7

Wren! Stop. Don't." He reached for the wooden box, but she got to it first and clutched it to her.

The powder puff flew out of his hand.

Lucinda caught it. "Cruel and selfish! You'd take away your sister's gift?" She gave the puff to Wren.

Effie feared for her son. "He's sorry, Lady Fairy. He didn't mean any harm, I'm sure."

"I certainly meant no harm," Milo said, trying diplomacy. "In my eyes—and the king's, I'm sure—Wren was just as she should be. Can't you put her hair back the way it was?"

"Milo!" Wren said.

Lucinda laughed, her good humor restored. "I *can*, but I *shan't*. Wait until she applies the cosmetics. You'll thank me then."

Wren took the wooden box to the dressing table, which had an ordinary mirror. She sat and picked up the powder puff.

"This is thrilling!" Lucinda said. "I wonder how the magic will interpret her."

Wren set down the puff. "Will you give Otto a mirror and cosmetics, too?"

"What a sweet dear," Lucinda said. "You want your love to benefit as you have."

Milo snorted—and disguised it as a sneeze.

"I do." She picked the powder puff up, then set it down again. "I can't do it with them here. Mother, Milo, would you wait outside?"

"Go on," Lucinda said. "Nothing bad can happen."

Milo wanted to refuse to leave—or to leave, saddle his horse, and ride home. But he followed his mother and stood with her in the corridor, held by curiosity and fear.

A sneak peek at
Gail Carson Levine's next novel,

A Tale of Two Castles

CHAPTER ONE

Mother wiped her eyes on her sleeve and held me tight. I wept onto her shoulder. She released me while I went on weeping. A tear slipped into the strait through a crack in the wooden dock. Salt water to salt water, a drop of me in the brine that would separate me from home.

Father's eyes were red. He pulled me into a hug, too. Albin stood to the side a few feet and blew his nose with a *honk*. He could blow his nose a dozen ways. A honk was the saddest.

The master of the cog called from the gangplank, "The tide won't wait."

I shouldered my satchel.

Mother began, "Lodie—"

"*E*lodie," I said, brushing away tears. "My whole name."

"Elodie," she said, "don't correct your elders. Keep your thoughts private. You are mistaken as often—"

"—as anyone," I said.

"Elodie . . . ," Father said, sounding nasal, "stay clear of the crafty dragons and the shape-shifting ogres." He took an uneven breath. "Don't befriend them! They won't bother you if you—"

"—don't bother them," I said, glancing at Albin, who shrugged. He was the only one of us who'd ever been in the company of an ogre or a dragon. Soon I would be near both. At least one of each lived in the town of Two Castles. The castle that wasn't the king's belonged to an ogre.

"Don't finish your elders' sentences, Lodie," Mother said.

"*E*lodie." I wondered if Father's adage was true. Maybe ogres and dragons bothered you *especially* if you didn't bother them. I would be glad to meet either one—if I had a quick means of escape.

Albin said, "Remember, Elodie: If you have to speak to a dragon, call it *IT*, never *him* or *her* or *he* or *she*."

I nodded. Only a dragon knows ITs gender.

Mother bent so her face was level with mine. "Worse than ogres or dragons . . . beware the whited sepulcher."

The whited sepulcher was Mother's great worry. I wanted to soothe her, but her instruction seemed impossible to follow. A sepulcher is a tomb. A whited sepulcher is someone who seems good but is, in truth, evil. How would I know?

"The geese"—Mother straightened, and her voice caught— "will look for you tomorrow."

The geese! My tears flowed again. I hated the geese, but I would miss them.

Mother flicked a gull's feather off my shoulder. "You're but a baby!"

I went to Albin and hugged him, too. He whispered into my hair, "Be what you must be."

The master of the cog roared, "We're off!"

I ran, leaped over a coil of rope, caught my foot, and went sprawling. Lambs and calves! Behind me, Mother cried out. I scrambled up, dusty but unharmed. I laughed through my tears and raced up the plank. A seaman drew it in.

The sail, decorated with the faded image of a winged fish, bellied in the breeze. We skimmed away from the dock. If fate was kind, in ten years I would see my parents and Albin again. If fate was cruel, never.

As they shrank, Mother losing her tallness, Father his

girth, Albin his long beard, I waved. They waved back and didn't stop. The last I could make out of them, they were still waving.

The island of Lahnt diminished, too. For the first time it seemed precious, with its wooded slopes and snowy peaks, the highest wreathed in clouds. I wished I could pick out Dair Mountain, where our Potluck Farm perched.

Farewell to my homeland. Farewell to my childhood.

Mother and Father's instructions were to apprentice myself to a weaver, but I would not. *Mansioner.* I mouthed the word into the wind, the word that held my future. *Mansioner.* Actor. Mansioner of myth and fable. Mother and Father would understand once I found a master or mistress to serve and could join the guild someday.

Leaning into the ship's hull, I felt the purse, hidden under my apron, which held my little knife, a lock of hair from one of Albin's mansioning wigs, a pretty pink stone, a perfect shell from the beach this morning, and a single copper, which Father judged enough to feed me until I became apprenticed. Unless the winds blew against us, we would reach Two Castles, capital of the kingdom of Lepai, in two or three days, in time for Guild Week, when masters took on new apprentices. I might see the king or the ogre, if one of them came through town, but I was unlikely to enter either castle.

I had no desire to see King Grenville III, who liked

war and taxes so much that his subjects called him Greedy Grenny. Lepai was a small kingdom, but bigger by half than when he'd mounted the throne—and so were our taxes bigger by half, or so Mother said. The king was believed to have his combative eye on Tair, Lahnt's neighbor across the wide side of the strait.

Queen Sofie had died a decade ago, but I did hope to see the king's daughter, Princess Renn, who was rumored to be somehow peculiar. A mansioner is interested in peculiarity.

And a mansioner observes. I turned away from home. To my left, three rowers toiled on a single oar. The one in the center called, "Pu-u-u-ll," with each stroke. I heard his mate across the deck call the same. Father had told me the oars were for steering and the sail for speed. The deck between me and the far hull teemed with seamen, passengers, a donkey, and two cows.

A seaman climbed the mast. The cog master pushed his way between an elderly goodman and his goodwife and elbowed the cows until they let him pass. He disappeared down the stairs to the hold, where the cargo was stored. I would remember his swagger, the way he rolled his shoulders, and how widely he stepped.

The deck tilted into a swell. I felt a chill, although the air was warm for mid-October.

"Go, honey, move. Listen to Dess. Listen, honey,

honey." A small man, thin but for fleshy cheeks and a double chin, the owner of the donkey and the cows, coaxed his animals into a space between the hull and the stairs to the rear upper deck. He carried a covered basket in his right hand, heavy, because his shoulder sagged. "Come, honey."

His speech reminded me of Father with our animals at home. *Good, Vashie,* he'd tell our cow, *Good girl, what a good girl.* Perhaps if I'd repeated myself with the geese, they'd have liked me better.

The elderly goodwife opened her sack and removed a cloak, which she spread on the deck. Holding her husband's hand, she lowered herself and sat. He sat at her side on the cloak. The other passengers also began to mark out their plots of deck, their tiny homesteads.

I wasn't sure yet where I wanted my place to be. Near the elderly couple, who might have tales to tell?

Not far from them, a family established their claim. To my surprise, the daughter wore a cap. In Lahnt women wore caps, but not girls, except for warmth in winter. Her kirtle and her mother's weren't as full as mine, but their sleeves hung down as far as their knuckles, and their skirt hems half covered their shoes, which had pointed toes, unlike my rounded ones.

The cog dropped into a slough in the sea, and my stomach dropped with it. We rose again, but my belly liked that no better. I leaned against the hull for better balance.

My mouth filled with saliva. I swallowed again and again. Nothing in the world was still, not the racing clouds nor the rippling sail nor the pitching ship.

The son in the family pointed at me and cried, "Her face is green wax!"

My stomach surged into my throat. I turned and heaved my breakfast over the side. Even after the food was gone, my stomach continued to rise and sink.

Next to me, a fellow passenger whimpered and groaned.

I stared down at the foamy water churning by, sicker than I had ever been. Still, the mansioner in me was in glory. Lambs and calves! I would remember how it was to feel so foul. I wondered if I could transform my face to green wax without paint, just by memory.

The cog rose higher than it had so far and fell farther. I vomited bile and then gasped for breath. The hull railing pressed into my sorry stomach.

The person at my side panted out, "Raise your head. Look at the horizon."

My head seemed in the only reasonable position, but I lifted it. The island of Lahnt had vanished. The horizon was splendidly flat and still. My insides continued bobbing, but less.

"Here." A hand touched mine on the railing. "Peppermint. Suck on it."

The leaf was fresh, not dried, and the clean taste helped. "Thank you, mistress." My eyes feared to let go of the horizon, so I couldn't see my benefactress. Her voice was musical, although not young. She might be the old goodwife.

"I've crossed many times and always begun by being sick." Her voice lilted in amusement. She seemed to have found respite enough from her suffering to speak more than a few words. I'm glad I looked. "I've exhausted my goodman's sympathy." She sighed. "I still hope to become a good sailor someday. You are young to travel alone."

Mother and Father didn't have passage money for more than me. "Not so young, mistress." Here I was, contradicting my elders again. "I am fourteen." Contradicting and lying.

"Ah."

I was tall enough for fourteen, although perhaps not curvy enough. I risked a sideways peek to see if she believed me, but she still faced the horizon and didn't meet my eyes. I took in her profile: long forehead, knob of a nose, weathered skin, deep lines around her mouth, gray wisps escaping her hood, a few hairs sprouting from her chin—a likeable, honest face.

"Conversation keeps the mind off the belly," she said,

and I saw a gap in her upper teeth.

The ship dropped. I felt myself go greener. My eyes snapped back to the horizon.

"We will be visiting our children and their children in Two Castles. Why do you cross?"

She was as nosy as I was! "I seek an apprenticeship as"—I put force into my hoarse, seasick voice—"a mansioner."

A Tale of Two Castles continues . . .

Experience these classics in a whole new way!

Gail Carson Levine's newest adventure!

ALSO AVAILABLE FROM GAIL CARSON LEVINE,
The Two Princesses of Bamarre AND *Fairest*

HARPER
An Imprint of HarperCollinsPublishers
www.booksandgames.com